# Steamtree
## The Airdrainium Adventures

## Brad R. Cook

A new series from the author of the Iron Chronicles

# Steamtree
The Airdrianium Adventures
Brad R. Cook



Published in the United States by Broadsword Books L.L.C.



ISBN: 978-0-9996433-0-3
Ebook ISBN: 978-0-9996433-1-0

www.bradrcook.com
@bradrcook

Cover and interior illustrations by Jennifer Stolzer
Jennifer Stolzer Illustrations www.jenniferstolzer.com
Interior and Cover Design by Brad R. Cook

Seriously, there are dragons and aircities in this book. If I missed this period of history, or if this exists today, please contact me

For

All the Tree Climbers

# The Airdrainium Adventures
## Book One

## Steamtree


## Brad R. Cook

# Chapter 1

I loved the smell and feel of wood, which was nothing like harsh, cold metal. Traders told tales of giants robed in leafy majesty, trees that stood taller than a building and thicker than a man. Aircities had shrubs they called trees, but the closest thing I'd ever touched were the squared off wooden boards and polished handrails on my parents' airship.

Leaning against the smooth wooden railing, the wind whipped my hair and tugged on my lifeline. The thick rope stretching between my belt and the rail kept me from blowing away. The goggles over my eyes blocked the wind's bitter sting and allowed me to see a rare sight – underneath the thick layer of puffy clouds covering the world. Today, patchy skies revealed an emerald sea of trees far below. I wanted nothing more than to climb one, or at least get close enough to see individual leaves.

I lived on the Caledonia. A dirigible or rigid airship, meaning it had a skeleton of metal ribbing covered in a tough canvas hull and armor plating over the important parts. Unlike a balloon, whose thin outer skin held nothing but hot air, the Caledonia had three decks, or floors, underneath several helium cells.

Segmented copper pipes wrapped around the aft section, or back half of the airship like the branches of a tree. These metal branches gripped the sides of the airship and cooled steam from the Airdrainium Boiler. Airdrainium Ore was the substance that made it possible to keep everything floating in the sky. Some pipes vented gases, while others acted as condensers and carried the heavy water infused with ore back to the engine room. I'd built a little fort in the branches of my steamtree. Okay, I had a lot of help, but this was *my* hideaway.

My fort had two parts. A tiny house made of reused wooden boards, scrap metal plating, and real glass portholes sat nestled among the pipes. With a sun deck laying on top of the pipes.

Standing on the deck, staring at the world below, revealed different colored strips of land with a meandering stream that dazzled in the sunlight. "Looks like dirters," I said aloud. That's what aircity dwellers called those left behind.

A roar, like a lion mixed with a trumpeting elephant, ripped through the noisy wind. I ran to the starboard side of the ship. Off in the distance, a column of thick, dark smoke rose through fluffy white clouds. My mind spun like a greasy gear trying to place what I'd heard. Certainly not thunder, or the Caledonia's engines. Fear mixed with my racing heart as I gripped the railing even tighter.

I twisted the only brass fixture holding the railing to the sundeck, and a board in the floor popped up to reveal a secret hiding spot. Several trinkets lay inside – my collection of pop bottle caps, a magnifying lens, and my compass. I pushed those aside and grabbed the monoscope Captain

Campbell gave me last year for my birthday.

Extending the brass tube, I raised the eyepiece to my goggles. With a few twists, I focused the lens on the thick black smoke. The churning column led down to a stone building atop a cliff with flames rising from the roof. Three ironclad zeppelins, twice the size of the Caledonia and armed with rows of cannons, hovered above the fire.

A deep voice echoed from below. "Master Greyvenhorn, are you anchored? The wind is wobblesmockin' today."

"Yes, Rohl," I said, lowering the monoscope. On the catwalk below, a man with a large belly and a big smile, waved. Along with a mom and a dad, I also had twelve crewmen who looked after me. I never minded. It meant fourteen presents on my birthday.

"Good," he said, and waved for me to come down. "Time to head inside." He scanned the skies and stared into the thick clouds, before turning back to me. Rohl cupped his hands around his mouth, "Your mother calls for you."

"I'll be right down." I knew I should tell her about the roar, so she could inform the captain. First, I needed to know I wasn't day dreaming. Again. I pointed toward the column of smoke. "Do you see it? I heard something, too."

A roar echoed in the distance. I peered through the lens. A dark shadow darted through the clouds. A flash drew my focus downward as a flaming war zeppelin plummeted from the sky and crashed into the cliff face. Moving the monoscope around, I saw only clouds and smoke. My heart sank. Those poor airmen.

One more time, I searched for whatever creature roared but didn't see anything. Something was out there, and I only had to find it. Inside the airship, my parents may not have heard the roar. Folding down the door created a short ladder from the sundeck into my steamtree fort. I unhooked my lifeline and stepped inside. Closing the door behind me silenced the noisy wind.

I tossed the monoscope into a canvas hammock that stretched from one wall to the other. A small bench and two portholes sat on the port side. I didn't have much furniture. My mom wouldn't let me live in my steamtree. I did have a great view of the sky and the Caledonia's catwalks. I lifted the elaborate brass hatch in the center of the floor. One of the mechanics made it. I climbed down onto a platform, closed the hatch, and pulled the key out of the center. Not a regular key, but a sprocket with missing teeth.

I slipped the key into my jacket pocket. A long, thin pipe stretched to the deck below. I grabbed hold, wrapped my legs around, and slid down. With a clatter, I landed on the grating below. The diamond-cut metal planks allowed rain and wind to pass through, and rattled as I ran off to find my parents.

Rohl held out his palm. "Five up-high."

I slapped his hand and ran toward the main hatch. "Did you see the smoke?"

He scratched his scraggily beard but kept watching the sky. "The Fleet must be dealing with dirters."

"There was something else in the clouds." I grabbed the handle and yanked up to open the hatch. "I gotta tell my parents."

"Don't worry; the captain will stay clear of those nasty plaguers." Rohl shaded his eyes with his hand to search the sky. "Get inside, now. I don't like that sound.

"Will do." I opened the door. "I think it was a dragon."

"Be quick about it," Rohl half-chuckled. "Never keep a lady waiting, especially your mother."

As I ran inside, the wind whipped my jacket against my back, and pushed me into Dogger, the head mechanic. A black cloud of soot enveloped us, but quickly blew away.

"Door," Dogger said as he pointed over my head.

"But I have to tell my parents about the..."

"Door."

"I was," I groaned. Struggling against the wind, I slammed the heavy door shut and it echoed through the corridor. My hands strained as I pushed the handle down into place. Dogger reached around me, but I quickly fired back, "I got it."

Dogger turned and grabbed a large wrench sticking off one of the interior pipes. Once the hatch was sealed, I waved, and ran off to find my mom.

The hallway ended at a bolted hatch with a sign overhead that read – *Helium Chamber*. I opened the door, and walked onto the long catwalks crossing through the center of the large open chamber. Above me, seven helium cells hung from the rafters, their seams strained to the point of bursting. They along with the Airdrainium ore, kept this craft in the sky. The airship's outer skin, a thick treated canvas, buffeted against the metal ribbing. The hum of the engine mixed with the whirring wind outside and echoed through the vast chamber, making this spot the noisiest place on the whole airship. I darted along the catwalk, swinging forward on the railing.

Spinning the metal handle, I yanked open the hatch to

the bow section, or front half of the ship, where my family lived. Quickly stepping inside, I shut the door, silencing the noises behind me. The cold metal planking disappeared behind beautiful rugs, painted walls, and real furniture. The living room had a large circular window on the starboard side, but I headed to my mother's workshop on the port side.

I stopped in front of her door, whipped off my goggles, and ran fingers through my hair like a comb, trying to smooth out every crazy strand. A soft but stern voice within said, "Anderax Grayvenhorn, enter this room. Immediately."

"Uh-oh, she used my first and last name, I'm in trouble." Not like when I left my dad's papers on the air dock—then she'd used all three of my names—but still, two names couldn't be good.

Running back to my steamtree sounded like a good plan, but she already knew I was here. If I did, I'd be in so much trouble she might put a Mister in front of all three names. I think that's why we have multiple names, so we know how much trouble we're in.

Snagging the door handle, I knew trouble would fade once she knew what I saw. "Coming."

I opened the door. My mom stood next to a dress form draped with cloth. She eyed me, her mouth squished to one side with pins held between her teeth. "Why are you sooty?"

"Must be from running into Dogger."

She made a swirling motion with her hand. "Step back. No dirty hands near Lady Skylark's dress." I backed into the living room. She stepped out and snagged my jacket's collar before I reached the couch. "Not so fast. Why are you in such a rush?"

"The sky. I saw something in the sky."

"Oh really? And what did you see?" She set the pins and swatch of cloth on her table and closed the door to her workshop. Spinning me around, she brushed dust from my shoulder.

"A dragon, I think. I heard a roar."

She tensed, then eased. "Are you certain it wasn't distant thunder?"

"Yeah, I saw fire and smoke."

"What?!" My mother gripped my shoulders. "What did you see?"

"Black smoke rising from the ground, and I heard a roar."

The seriousness of her eyes made me wonder if I'd said something wrong.

My father walked out of his office and shook his head. "He didn't actually see anything, probably just a trick of the wind."

I shrugged. "Something took out that airship."

My mother and father eyed each other.

"To be safe." Her smile faded. "Why don't you stay inside until we get to the aircity."

# Chapter 2

I asked my mother, "Have you ever seen a dragon?"

"Aye, I have."

"Whoa," I leaned closer. "What are they like? Why don't we see them? Where do they come from?" I had a thousand more questions, but my mother had a distant, far away stare, and my father's face soured.

"Plaguer beasts. Foul creatures of myth." My father shook his head. "Aja, do not fill his head with fantasies. They're all gone." He came and knelt down in front of me, as if trying to reach my level, but he looked so stiff and awkward. "We must be wary of the ground, for the plagues still ravage the dirters. Two hundred years ago our ancestors left the ground to populate the sky. Clean air and sunshine over the dreary and stinky land below."

"But, the trees."

"Everything we need can be grown here in the clouds, including wood." He stood and walked over to the window. Staring at the endless puffy cloudscape, he never even glanced at the ground. "We've traveled throughout the western skies and never had a problem with myths. Aja, let's not give him nightmares."

She didn't say anything.

My father walked over to a small table in the center of the room. The polished-wood top ringed a collection of brass tubes running from the floor to the ceiling. He dipped his quill in the inkwell and penned a note on a small piece of parchment. Selecting one of the brass-and-glass vials arranged in a metal and velvet stand, he slipped the paper inside and sealed the container. The whine of rushing air filled the room as he opened one of the tubes. He placed the container inside and sealed the end. With a "whoomp," the message zipped up the tube.

I knew the message would pop out on the bridge, but wondered what it said.

My mother brushed off my jacket. "We will be arriving in Londaria later today. You should have completed your reports for the tutor, but when I checked, they were half-finished. Now, march yourself into the bathroom and then straight to work."

"Can you help me?"

"I have to finish this dress, or Duchess Skylark will have nothing to wear. Wouldn't that be scandalous?" Her smile lit up the room, and she playfully ruffled my unruly hair.

I kicked the corner of the rug with my boot. "I'll finish them."

"Thank you, my little man." She knelt down. "I know homework is no fun, but learning is. Get cleaned up, and I mean scrub good. Then bring your reports to my workshop, and we'll do them together."

I nodded and ran to my room.

Returning well washed, with homework in hand, I flopped on the coiled rug in my mom's workshop. I spread the papers out in an arc. Math was never fun. I liked history. Tales of great warriors and exciting stories. My tutor said math would be more helpful, but I didn't believe him. My father used math all the time. However, the last thing I wanted was to become an air inspector. I liked traveling to all the air-cities, but constantly leaving made it hard to keep friends.

My mother continued sewing at a machine on her desk. Layers of silken fabric filled her lap as she fed the bundle toward the needle. Her smile melted my worries away.

When she glanced at me I asked, "What makes an angle acute?"

"It's good to see every angle," she winked, "but acute means smaller than ninety degrees."

I worked on my studies until she'd finished the hi-noble-woman's dress.

My father entered wearing the same long black coat and light grey slacks he wore every day. Grabbing the back of my mother's chair, he kissed her on the cheek. Then he leaned over my shoulder and smiled. "Math, my favorite subject." I groaned, and he eyed me through the round frames of his glasses. "Math will serve you throughout your life."

With a heavy sigh, I nodded.

"A civilized world is defined by its parameters."

*Oh no, not another lecture.* My father could talk about nothing for hours. I tried to think of a way out, but I was trapped.

"Those parameters must be measurable." He continued, pacing back and forth in front of me. "The measurements must be recorded so they can be turned into facts that can be used to calculate and postulate the future. Such is math."

"Math tells the future?" I had no idea what postu...whatever meant, but I was pretty sure math was a mind-crushing amount of numbers.

"Kind of, but math is so much more."

"I don't know how math is going to help me fight a drag-on."

"That's not something you'll have to deal with, so I wouldn't worry about it."

"But I saw..."

Mutt, the cabin boy, rushed in holding a folded piece of paper in his hand. He was older than me, but he was the youngest member of the Caledonia's crew. My father turned and motioned for him to come over.

"Urgent message from the captain, sir. The reports from Londaria came over the wire." Mutt held out the paper.

My father took the note and read it several times. His brow scrunched together and his fingers traced his chin. "This can't be right."

Mutt stood at attention. "Capt'n wanted me to say…message was confirmed, sir."

"I need to check these numbers." He stepped out of his office, and the cabin boy left. I heard my father shuffling papers. He stormed back in. "Dear, you'll never believe this. Why I'm not sure I even believe it."

"What is it?" My mother looked up from her dress form.

"If these numbers are correct—which I will have to verify once we arrive—Londaria has dropped three feet."

I shrugged my shoulders. "That's doesn't sound like very much."

"A few inches are tolerable, but a foot, never. And three feet!" My father shook his head so hard, his glasses slid to the end of his nose. "Why…Londaria hasn't moved three feet in two hundred years."

My mother returned to her dress form. "That does sound serious. Maybe the numbers are wrong."

"They have to be."

I pointed to my books. "So, the math isn't adding up?"

"I must confirm these numbers." He walked out of the workshop, barely acknowledging me. My mother followed, leaving me alone with my books.

A glass-and-brass vial zipped back through the pneumatic tubes in the center of the room. Each tube had a section that ended in a screw cap. Some pointed up and were made to send messages, others pointed down and received messages. I walked over and slid open the end, air rushed out, and I grabbed the container. A message lay inside. I knew it was for my father, but wanted to know what it said.

I opened the brass-and-glass vial, and unrolled the parchment. The captain had written back to my father –

*Yes, dragon spotted. We will make Londaria without issue.*

"I knew it! Dragons *are* real."

# Chapter 3

Soft footsteps outside this room made me slip back to my reports and stuff the note between the pages of my books. My mother poked her head back into her studio. "We'll be docking soon. Why don't you wear the new suit I made you?"

"I will." Scooping up my books, I ran into living room. She kissed the top of my head, and spun around to lock the door. Placing her hand on my back, she escorted me to my room. "Can I go to market square? Please." I hoped using the magic word might get a yes.

"We will see, but first you must be on your best behavior at your father's welcoming ceremony. Afterward, we are expected at Duke Skylark's estate. He is hosting all of us."

That sounded like a lot of boring standing around. "Is that the same place we stayed before? With all the beautiful birds in cages."

"No. Duchess Skylark requested a dress, and the Duke was gracious enough to host us. This will not be like the nobles we usually stay with, the Skylarks are hi-nobility, expect the seriousness of LuftBerlin and the grandeur of Romaria."

"Will we get to see the Queen?"

Her grip on my shoulder tightened as her nails dug into

my skin. Looking up, I saw a distant stare, as if she was look-ing right through the wall. I twisted away from the pain. She instantly pulled away her hand, and stepped back. "We're not important enough to visit with her Highness. However, I'm certain she'll read your father's reports."

"That is important."

"Well, she'll have one of her ministers read and summa-rize it to her, but yes, your father is an important man."

"Everything's okay with Londaria, right?"

"Of course."

"So, the numbers were off?"

"What?"

"I don't want to be on Londaria if it's falling."

"The city is not falling. It is lower than it should be. The engineers are probably using too thin of an airdrainium mix-ture."

We walked down the hall and entered my bedroom, the last door on the portside. My parents' chamber was on the starboard side and filled the entire bow, or front of the air-ship. My mother decorated my room to match the night's sky with stars and clouds painted on the walls and ceiling. Rugs covered the floor, and several chests were braced to one wall so they wouldn't slide around when the Caledonia passed through choppy weather.

"Now come on, we can't be late." She flipped open one trunk lid, pulled my suit out, and laid it on my bed. "I have to get ready, so hurry up and I'll meet you on the landing deck." She rushed out of my room.

Chains anchored my brass barrel-bed to the ceiling and floor. It meant no matter the airship's angle, I slept smoothly through the night. I swung around the chain and spun off past my desk with a built-in chair, landing at my favorite spot – two portholes in a cushioned alcove. Exactly the same as in my steamtree. Best of all, I could look forward or aft.

I changed into the suit, and slipped on my goggles. I didn't like going anywhere without my goggles. How was I supposed to see?

The door opened and Rohl stepped inside. "I've come to take you to the landing platform, Master Grayvenhorn."

I stared down at the dark suit. "Do I look like a gentleman?"

He leaned back and nodded. "A right-proper honorable gent indeed."

I smiled.

He motioned over his shoulder. "Your father's asking for yah."

"On my way!" I gave a quick salute and ran out of my room toward the stairs. I'd learned last year if I grabbed the railing on each side, and hooked my feet on the lower runner, I could slide down without having to use the steps. Once at the bottom, I let go and ran across the deck. My father eyed me, I don't think he liked my move, but my mother smiled and pulled me to her side.

She knelt down, being careful to avoid crumpling her dress. She straightened my hair by running her fingers through it, and pointed to my neck. "Where's the tie?"

"In my pocket." I pulled out a tangled tie-ball.

"Well, it's not doing any good in your pocket. Give it here. She slipped the silk around my neck and tied it in an elaborate knot. Bound in layered wool, I stretched, pulled and worked my fingers between suit and skin. I never liked suits, too similar to a straight-jacket.

My mother smoothed out my shoulders, nudged me, and whispered, "Quit fidgeting."

"I can't breathe."

"Don't be so dramatic. In this corset, I'm far worse than you." She kissed the top of my head, and we joined my father who stood before the outer hatch practicing his lines.

Through the window, Londaria grew ever larger. As with all aircities, they appeared to float along nestled atop the clouds. The city was an exact replica of Old London, including the river. "I see the Thames."

My father leaned closer and nodded. "Two hundred years ago they took the best of what remained in the cities, and brought them into the sky."

"Why not lift everyone up?"

My father chuckled. He dropped his hand on my shoulder, and laughed with the captain. "Why there'd never be enough airdrainium. The ore that powers the aircities. All those people would be too heavy. They'd never lift them all." He turned to Captain Campbell, "You see, this is why you need children, to bring a moment of levity to every situation."

The captain nodded. "Of course, Inspector Grayvenhorn."

My father let me go, but I still wanted an answer. I didn't think it was a silly question.

The city of polished brass and silver gleamed in the sunlight. Airships from around the world perched like birds on a branch along the air docks.

The Caledonia soared up to the main docking hanger.

Dogger popped open a hatch, while two crewmen cranked a wheel to feed the heavy twisted rope out of the side of the airship. The mooring lines uncoiled and linemen rushed across the docks. They hooked the cable to a large geared-spool and cranked us in the rest of the way.

The captain leaned down. "Here lad, you'll want to see the docking clamps secure the ship. He pointed out the window." A large pair of metal fingers rotated at the end of an iron-riveted docking arm and locked onto the nose of our airship. "Once secured, the Caledonia will not budge." Dogger and Rohl extended the gangplank and secured the metal walkway. Then the captain spun around on his heel and bowed to my father. "The vessel is secured, sir. Welcome to Londaria."

"Thank you, Captain Campbell." My father bowed his head. "We will see you in five days. Make certain the ship is ready to depart."

"Of course, sir."

I followed my mother down the gangplank to the docks. Through the metal grating, I saw the billowing clouds below. My father moved quickly to the solid planking at the end of the dock. He didn't like looking down, but I did. So much space below. I wanted to fly through all of it, but I didn't have wings.

"Stay by my side," my mother said extending her lace covered hand. "The docks are no place to be reckless."

I wanted to protest. I was eleven, and therefore not a baby anymore. I knew the docks could be dangerous, but I'd been on them my whole life. I knew what to do.

Several screams escaped the airship next to ours and erased

all the reckless thoughts from my mind. Painful cries made me shudder as if standing in a winter's breeze. A grimy man in a dark suit leapt from the airship's deck into the coiled rope below. He popped up and sprinted toward the city, but a winged-man soared overhead. The man in the suit stopped. He raised a bloody short sword and a flint-lock pistol.

I tugged my mother's arm and pointed at the winged man, "An archangel."

"Yes." Her hand trembled with mine inside.

Large, mechanical wings moved with rhythmic grace. Gears turned bronze articulated arms with white feathers layered into brass fittings. The archangel's shoulder length dark hair whipped about his serene yet stern expression. His long white coat buckled at the shoulder, and leather straps wound around his chest to hold a large white orb that gleamed in the light. Everyone on the docks stopped to stare.

The archangel swooped down and landed. Mechanical wings folded down along his back. He stared at the man in the suit, not saying a word. The man stepped back, stumbling over his boots. He raised his pistol and fired, but the archangel spun to the side, easily avoiding the bullet.

My mother clutched me close. Her arm pressed against my chest. I struggled to see over her sleeve. She pulled me toward my father, but never turned her back on the archangel. I tried to wiggle free, but she gripped me tighter.

The man in the suit waved the bloody short sword, but the archangel's expression never changed. The only thing that moved were his all-white eyes that studied his opponent's movements.

In a deep voice that echoed off the airships, the archangel

said, "Your first mistake was killing the captain of that vessel. Your second was thinking you wouldn't have to pay for that crime."

The man in suit frantically screamed, "I had too, that—"

"Judgement – Guilty!" The archangel thrust his hand forward. His fingertips and the orb on his chest glowed with a smoldering orange light. He snatched his hand closed, and wrenched the man's soul out of his body. A ghostly spirit, the same shape as the man only made of transparent energy, flailed his arms and legs. The body tried to grip the energy, but his fingers slipped right through. The archangel split the spirit from the body, and the man in the suit slumped to the ground. Particles of light disappeared on the wind.

I froze and my stomach slammed into the pit of my stomach. I had never seen anything so terrifying. I didn't know if I'd ever sleep again.

My mother dropped down and tried to engulf me, but she was too late. I couldn't take my eyes off the archangel. Something in his all white eyes disturbed me. Joy. He'd enjoyed ripping that guy's soul. I didn't like that.

My mother ushered me over to my father who looked on with apathy. His focus lay not on the angel flying off, but on locating the city officials.

"Did you see that?" I gripped my chest. "My soul can't fall out, right?"

My father scoffed. "Of course not. Only the evil need fear. Now, this is not the time for such nonsense."

My mother bent down and took my cheeks in her hands. "You have nothing to worry about." She'd stopped trembling. I wish I could. Her soft smile helped. "Anderax, there are better ways to deal with any situation. I'm sorry you had to see that."

My father pulled my mother up. "Come now, both of you. It was just an archangel dealing with a criminal. Hardly something worth more than a moment's thought."

"Of course, dear." My mother's voice hardened.

I didn't think so. The archangels defended every aircity, and this was the first one I had ever seen up close, but something didn't seem fair. He didn't listen to that man, or even ask a single question.

"Come, the Lord High Chancellor is right over there." My father ruffled my hair, and I crossed my arms, annoyed.

"Inspector Greyvenhorn," the Lord High Chancellor said. He wore elaborate black robes and a funny hat, but the gold rings on his fingers were the biggest I had ever seen.

My father bowed. "Lord High Chancellor Rycroft, thank you for meeting me. It is an honor."

The Lord High Chancellor cleared his throat. "Allow me to introduce Duke Skylark." He motioned to the man beside him, who looked younger than I would have thought a duke. Though, his chin rose the appropriate amount for a noble. His sky-blue suit trimmed with gold and lace, had the flair of old-world nobility, rather than the simpler suits of common men.

My father bowed. "Thank you for hosting us, Milord."

"Of course. Besides, my wife eagerly awaits this dress."

My mother curtsied and smiled behind her hand. "You are too kind. I truly hope she enjoys it."

"I as well. Though I'm certain she will." The Duke smiled.

Lord High Chancellor Rycroft clapped his hands together.

"I'm glad this meeting has gone so well. Inspector, please enjoy the Duke's hospitality. We will discuss your visit soon enough."

My father nodded. "I am eager to start my inspections."

The Lord High Chancellor nodded and stepped away as the Duke motioned with his hand. "My carriage is right this way, and my estate awaits."

# Chapter 4

The Duke's carriage didn't have wheels, but hovered a few feet off the street. In all my travels I'd never seen one more lavish. "How does it do that?"

"Airdrainium. The clouds underneath give it away." My father pointed at the puffy white cushion clinging to the underside of the brass and polished black lacquer carriage.

"Like the aircities and the Caledonia." I stopped in front of the mechanical steed. "This isn't a real horse." Iron legs rose to a body plated with silver and gold. Through the seams I saw gears and pistons moving inside.

"It's an automaton." My father shook his head, looking annoyed with his brow all scrunched up. "A machine that mimics a real animal."

"Like the peacock that served tea at the museum in Paris de l'aire?"

"That's right." My mother smiled, put her hand on my back, and led me to the carriage.

I climbed inside and ran my hand along the plush velvet that covered the seat and walls. My mother followed, and my father sat beside her. The Duke sat across from us on the other bench, watching me with a weird little smirk on his face. To avoid him, I stared out the window which was way more interesting than their boring conversation.

Buildings of brick, brass, iron, and steel rose up along winding cobblestone streets. The further we traveled, the taller the buildings became, until we reached the central tower, Big Bend. The whole aircity spun on this axis, like a top. Every city had one. I liked Londaria's giant clock, more than Romaria's Trajan's Column.

Duke Skylark asked my father, "I trust your journey was a pleasant one."

My father nodded. "We've arrived from Paris de l'aire. We enjoyed a sunny trip over the channel."

The nobleman tugged at his sleeves. "Ah yes, those infernal Culturalist's always wanting to put on some new production when important work needs attention. Tell me, had the Nightraven appeared lately?"

I turned from the window. "What's a Nightraven?"

The Duke's eyes narrowed as his fist clenched. I guess he didn't like me speaking. My father started to apologize, but the nobleman raised his hand. "Not a what, but a who."

I scratched my head, "What who?"

Seeing my confusion, the Duke continued, "A dangerous thief who has struck many of the aircities."

A dangerous thief sounded exciting. "Who is he?"

"No one knows, but worry not, the archangels will catch him."

I raised my hand, "I have a question?"

My parents cringed and the Duke took a deep breath. "Yes."

"Where do archangels comes from?" I crossed my arms getting in my best thinking pose. "They don't look like real angels."

My mother smiled, but hid it behind a handkerchief. The vein on the side of my father's neck bulged out and turned red as he twisted in his seat.

The Duke smiled. "An inquisitive youth. You'll be a fine inspector one day." He reached over and ruffled my hair. I froze. I hated when people did that to me. Besides, I didn't want to be like my father. He'd never climbed a tree.

My father shook his head. "I guess his tutor has yet to cover the archangels, I will rectify that when I see him."

The Duke pointed out of the window. A large cathedral with tall pointy spires rose above all the surrounding buildings. "Archangels are our protectors. They serve the Cardinal, and have power over life and death. Be thankful for them, they are the only ones who can defeat a dragon."

My eyes popped open. "Wow."

"Yes, they are very, wow." The Duke turned up his nose. "Ah, we are here, thank the winds."

I pressed against the glass. Bushes lined the edge of a grassy patch with a large mansion rising out of the center. "Your house is in a park?"

My father took in a deep breath through clenched teeth.

My mother leaned closer, "These are the Duke's personal grounds. That's enough questions for now. Save them for later."

No more questions, but what about the designs on the Duke's front gate. A dragon wrapped in roses. I'd seen the emblem in my school books. I'd have to make a list of everything I wanted to know.

*What was with all the white stone statues on the Duke's grounds?*

*Who were they?*
*Why did the Duke live in such a big house?*
*Oh yeah, and then the dragon design on the door.*
I might need to write them down.

The carriage stopped and we slipped out. Before me stood two large wooden doors with bronze roses wrapped around a golden dragon. I followed my mother, father, and the Duke as they entered the house and crossed the polished marble floor. The Duke spun on his heel. "Welcome to Rosecliff. My home is your home. The servants have already made arrangements for your belongings. This is Wadsworth, my butler. He will show you to your rooms."

An older man, buttoned up in a black and white suit stepped up. "Of course, sir. Walk this way."

For a moment I wanted to copy his shuffling gate, but my dad was already annoyed. I'd get sent back to the Caledonia for certain, and not in a good way. I'd be locked in my room. The thought of missing these boring events made me consider it, but one sharp glance from my mother, and I followed them.

We walked along plush carpets, through hallways filled with portraits and statues. Each painting held a different hi-noble in regal dress. Then we walked down a hall lined with suits of armor. My favorite, so far.

*Another question. Who were all the people in these weird paintings?*

As we reached the end of the hall, a huge portrait dominated the wall. Duke Skylark sat on a horse with his sword raised. We turned down another short hallway and Wadsworth stopped in front of a series of doors. "These are your chambers. The master suite is for you and your wife, sir.

The room across the hall is for the ward, and," he pointed at a third door, "We've converted the study into a studio."

He opened the door to the master suite, and my parents entered. The cavernous room could fit three of the Caledonia's rooms, or more. Everything inside held the luxury of ornate and overly decorated items, even the bed was trimmed with gold. On the Caledonia weight always factored into anything, decorations tended to be plain.

My mother walked me across the hall to my room. Knights on horseback in some kind of parade had been painted on the walls. "Who are all these people?"

"See the one in front? What does his shield hold?"

"A gold dragon."

"That's Arthur Pendragon, a legendary King of Britain. He forged peace on the land below us."

"Wow." I ran my hand over all the men in armor behind him. "These must be the Knights of the Round Table."

"My little man is so smart."

I smiled.

A large wooden bed filled with pillows dominated the room. Elaborately carved swirls, various fruit, and small animals filled every inch. I'd never seen so much wood, and couldn't stop running my fingers over all the lines. My trunk had already been placed at the end of the bed. My mother opened it, and pulled out a suit. "I want you to wear this to diner."

I groaned. "I have to change again?"

"Yes, and you have to be on your best behavior tonight."

"I'll try."

She left the room, and I went to the window.

# Chapter 5

My usual blue-sky view had been replaced by buildings lining the New Thames River as it wound through the center of the city. The only sky lay above me, and still not a single tree in sight. I stepped away from the window and finally changed suits, right before my mother called me.

Wadsworth led us to the dining room. A long narrow table with thin high-backed chairs, filled the chamber. Each seat was marked by a small card with our names, pinned in place by the thorn of a golden rose. I sat in the middle next to my mother. My father sat beside the Duke at the end of the table.

I wanted to ask my questions. I had a list, but every time I started to talk, my mother would touch my leg and I'd stop.

They served soup first, but it tasted funny, and I only swished the liquid around in the decorative silver bowl. I didn't even recognize the next two dishes, and wondered if I'd be able to eat anything. My stomach grumbled, but my mouth still refused to take a bite.

The Duke announced to the table, "Those pesky dirter attacks have left us without olive oil. Do pardon any taste issues. Chef did what he could."

My ears perked up. Dirters. I wanted to know more.

A man, his chest decorated in more medals and ribbons, than any other guest, slammed the table. "Those demons need to be dealt with once and for all."

"Agreed Admiral." The Duke raised his glass. "Inspector, didn't you encounter something on your way here."

My father dabbed the corner of his mouth with his napkin. "There was a large fire to the east."

The Duke nodded. "Ah yes, the cleansing of the abbey." He turned to a few other men sitting across from me. "Lord High Chancellor Rycroft was telling me, they destroyed a suspected Dragonrider Den. The Admiral can probably tell us more."

The Admiral leaned back, and laughed. I thought he might fall over from the weight on his chest. "Yes, the dragons flew off in fear. They did get one airship, but the royal fleet has them on the run now."

"I saw it." I announced over my mother's pinching objection. "A dragon flew down and destroyed one of the war zeps."

Everyone stared at me. The whole table went silent and stopped eating. The Duke turned to my father who bowed his head, and then turned to stare at me with anger spilling from his eyes. The rest of his face though held only a nobleman's stoic expression.

I wished I'd stayed quiet.

"Allow me to introduce the Inspector's son." The Duke eyed me. "Tell me, do you like dragons, or fear them?"

"I thought they were myth, until today." I hesitated and glanced at my mother, she nodded. I said, "But, I like them.

They fly."

The Admiral slammed the table rattling the plates and goblets. "They're demons!"

The Duke smiled. "He is a boy and cannot fathom the world he is in. Much like a baby."

My face scrunched up. I didn't like being called a baby. I didn't know how to react. I wanted to say something. I wanted to tell him that I thought dragons would kick his airships right out of the sky, but I held my tongue.

The admiral laughed. "Well there's nothing to worry about, the new dreadnaughts will hunt down those demons and their riders."

Dragons had riders?

No one told me dragons had people who rode them. Who were they? Where did they come from? I wanted to know, but even this *baby* knew to keep my interest in the enemy to myself.

The Duke nodded. "Yes, I'm certain the new strategies and airships have turned the tide."

My mother said, "I would be happy to see peace. This war has raged my whole life."

Duchess Skylark's soft voice swept in from the other end of the table. "This war is never-ending. Why do you think we sought refuge in the sky? The dragons caused the plagues which ravaged humanity, then those beasts fed off the dead. I am with the Admiral. This war will only end when the demons are eliminated. Let them have the ground, who needs it, we are stupendous in our air-bound cities."

The Duke smiled. "Such talk at diner. Forgive me, dear. Matters of state should be left to gentlemen in a ministry meeting, not at dinner. I assure you all with the Admiral guarding the dreadnaught's secrets, we have nothing to fear."

Right as this boring party was getting interesting, the Duchess raised her glass, "Enough of this disturbing subject. I wish to toast. To the health of her Highness!"

"Long live the Queen!" Everyone said in unison as they lifted their goblets.

I didn't know what to say, so I stayed silent. Besides, I knew no one wanted to hear from me. My mother didn't say anything either. Her mouth moved and she raised her glass, but I couldn't hear her.

Duchess Skylark set down her glass. "Thank you all. I'm sure her Highness appreciates our support. Now, I must move on to important matters. For those who don't know, Inspector Grayvenhorn's wife is a dress maker and I wish to see my new gown."

The Duke raised his glass. "My wife has spoken, and this dinner is over. Gentlemen, if you will join me in parlor, as the ladies take over the salon."

The Duke looked so smug, and treated everyone like we were children. At least it wasn't only me. I wanted to follow my father. Maybe the admiral would talk more about the war, or dragons, but my mother snagged my shoulder and dragged me off with her.

We entered a brightly lit room with walls covered in painted pastel flowers. Wooden furniture covered in silken fabric created a circle in the center of the room. All the women gathered and sat with the Duchess in the center. My mother pointed to a chair against the wall. "Dock yourself."

I knew what she meant. She'd spotted my prison cell and

if my tush left the assigned seat, I'd never sit down again. "Okay. Can I–"

"No. I have to show the Duchess her dress. You sit and stay silent." She left the room, but came back a moment later leading two servants struggling with a large trunk.

The Duchess began to clap. She and her friends squealed with delight and bounced in their chairs. My mother had the two men it tight suits set the trunk down. She opened it and lifted the dress.

"Oh! It is beautiful." The Duchess covered her heart. "Look at the embellishments."

Two noblewomen sitting beside her piped up in unison, "It is so you. The whole court with die from envy."

My mother had one of the servants set up a dress form as she fitted the gown onto it. She then stepped back allowing the women admire the gown. They rushed forward, running their fingers over the fabric and along the stitching. I didn't see why they made such a fuss, all I saw was an ocean of layered silks rippling like waves.

Several women demanded a dress from my mother, but the Duchess silenced them with a wave of her hand. "Ladies, may I remind you that Aja is a guest in my house." She smiled. "She will be making dresses for *me*."

All the noblewomen laughed and my mother bowed graciously.

One woman with blue ribbons woven in her hair, Lady Kingfisher, leaned in to the Duchess. "The Nightraven is certain to try and steal it."

The Duchess laughed. "I'll have to start locking them away with my jewels."

My mother smiled. "Thank you. You're too kind."
If the Nightraven appeared, at least that would be exciting.

# Chapter 6

A rapidly ringing bell outside my window ripped me from my dream. I rubbed my eyes, jumped out of bed, and ran to the glass. Whistles echoed through the night as constables frantically searched the surrounding streets, and a pair of archangels circled above.

Hearing voices in the hall, I tip-toed over and pressed my ear against the door. Two men spoke to my father in a serious tone. One grumbled in a thick accent, "Sir, remain in here. We've 'ad reports of the Nightraven."

In Londaria? I wanted to run out and find this thief. What might he be trying to steal, money, jewelry, or could he really be after my mother's dresses?

My father sounded annoyed. "What is this business with the Nightraven? I had to deal with this in Paris de l'aire as well."

In a much deeper voice, the second man said, "There isn't an aircity the Nightraven hasn't swindled. Nobody knows who he is, but he stands against the Queen and her ministers."

"A black feather tis 'is calling card," added the first man.

*A black feather marking each theft — how had I not known. I was in Paris de l'aire.*

"I do hope you catch him," my father said. "But must you disturb *me* for this?"

The second man said, "Duke's orders are to investigate everything. Someone at the house tonight was robbed."

"Who?" My father asked.

The first man replied, "Can't tell yah, sir."

The Duke was worried at dinner about the Nightraven finding the Admiral's plans. However, if it was the Duchess' dress then the thief might come here. However, they said the Nightraven hadn't been in the house, so I doubted it was the dress.

A stern tone came to the second guard's voice, "Remain here. The constables might have questions for you."

My father said, "I understand. Of course, we will cooperate."

They must have left because everything went silent. I slipped back to the window just as an archangel flew past. He soared between the buildings and hovered at the end of the block. His mechanical wings flapped majestically, pausing for a moment, before darting down another street and disappearing behind the buildings.

The door to the bathroom swung open, crying on rusty hinges. My mother stepped through, her arms stretched over her head as she finished tying her corset. "You should be in bed, young man."

"I can't, this is exciting." I leaned around her, wondering where she came from.

My mother quickly shuffled me toward the bed. "I was in my workroom. The bathroom connects the two."

"Is that where the door went?"

"That's right." She pulled my arms out of my pajamas and grabbed another set from my trunk.

I didn't know why I needed to change, but I lifted the shirt over my head. A loud knock at the door made me jump. My mother took a deep breath. She walked over to the door, but paused to smooth out her dress and fix her hair. Then she opened the door.

A constable filled the doorway, shiny silver buttons dazzled like stars against his black uniform. A tall rounded-hat towered over me as he bowed. "Pardon me mam, I have a few questions to ask you about the incident tonight."

"What has happened?"

I looked at her. How did she miss everything?

The constable's face hardened. "The Nightraven struck the Admiral's house."

My mother's hand covered her heart, her mouth dropped open, and she stepped back. "Oh my, is everyone okay? He was just at dinner speaking ill of that rogue."

"Luckily, the Admiral defended his family and fought off the intruder."

"Really." Her stance hardened, but then she relaxed. "How heroic."

"I'm afraid I've been ordered to account for everyone. Forgive the question, but where were you over the last hour?"

I expected her to say, her workroom, but without missing a beat, she smiled and said, "Getting my son ready for bed."

That wasn't the truth. My father always said I was to tell the truth to authorities like the constable. I didn't say anything, I wasn't going to rat out my mother. At least that's what the Caledonia's crew would say.

"Thank you, mam. That's all I need. You both have a good night." He bowed and turned away.

My mother shut the door. She let out a long sigh and turned to me with a big smile. "Well, it certainly has been an exciting evening. Come on let's get you into bed and I'll read you a story."

As I pulled on my nightshirt I thought about the Nightraven. Who was this master thief and what did he want? Another archangel flew past the window. They weren't giving up. He must still be out there. "Who is the Nightraven?"

She paused, then sat on the bed's side rail. "Why do you want to know about this thief?"

"The Nightraven sounds fascinating."

She drew back four layers of cloud-like down covers. "Let's talk about this tomorrow. Which book do you want me to read from?"

"The Scarlet Pimpernel."

# Chapter 7

About mid-morning my mother came in, "Time to get ready for lunch."

"No yet…"

"Take a bath, and be certain to scrub. Then you'll have to get into a fine suit." I groaned, but she said. "We're having lunch with the Duchess."

"When do we depart Londaria?"

She brushed off my suit. "Not for a few more days, aren't you having fun?"

"No."

"I guess we do need to do more kids activities, but we're with the hi-nobles. Life is dictated by the royal schedule."

"Can we see the rest of Londaria? Maybe play on the grounds?"

"No, you can't enter the grounds. They're not for tearing up."

"Can we at least get out of this place? It feels like a museum. Oh, can we go to the Caledonia?"

She shook her head. "I know this isn't the most exciting place, but your father has to be here and so must we."

I groaned, and ran into the giant marble bathroom.

* * *

My mother tugged and tucked every piece of clothing I wore. I struggled to breathe and crossed my arm. She led me to the front hall. Two servants in shiny jackets and tight leggings stood ready to open the door.

The Duchess descended the stairs as if on a cloud. Her elegant yellow dress swished back and forth like the brush strokes of a painting. "I love your suit, such a dapper young man." I squirmed and she turned to my mother. "He's a perfect little gentleman. The Princess will love you both."

"Her highness is going to be there?" My mother snapped her head up. "I thought she'd declined."

"Her schedule has freed up, and I intend to speak to her about your dresses."

My mother smiled nervously. "You are too kind."

The Duchess clutched her hands together. "Your dresses are works of art. The Princess will adore them."

My mother bowed and Duchess Skylark motioned us toward the garden. In the center of tall green hedges and short stone walls sat a gazebo with tables underneath. Rose bushes ringed the stones columns and steps, and the green grass surrounded us like a lake. The strong aroma knocked me over. I was used to grease, burning coal, and metal. Not fresh-cut grass or thorn-covered roses. I dropped to my knees and pressed my palms into the trimmed lawn. "It tickles." The cool ground felt like metal planking in the morning.

My mother rushed to my side and pulled me up. "What did I tell you about the grounds!"

The Duchess giggled. "Oh, it's quite all right. Growing boys need room to spread out."

My mother curtsied, flaring out the bottom of her dress.

"He's never been to the ground. You are too generous."

"Who needs the ground anyway?" The Duchess giggled. "Come, the ladies of my Whist Club are joining us in the gazebo."

I wanted to protest and tell her about trees, but my mother pulled me behind the Duchess. I stepped on the grass which was spongy, not like solid metal. I bounced with each step.

My mother let go of my hand as she and the Duchess stepped up into the gazebo. I bolted for the hedge row. They weren't trees, but were made of wood, and smelled so divine. I ran straight into a mass of branches which snagged my jacket and shirt. The soft pointy needles poked against my face, and I laughed.

Inside lay a web of interlocking branches too thin to climb. As I reached deeper, the leaves that thickly covered the outside vanished. I wrapped my fingers around rough twigs, not like the smooth wood that covered the Caledonia's decks. There was something else, something subtle – the wood – pulsed with life.

"Anderax Greyvenhorn, get out of the hedges and come here." My mother's voice cut through my joy like a sword.

I pulled back and brushed the needles off my jacket. "Coming."

As I reached the gazebo, my mother's expression hardened, but the rest of the ladies, giggled and spoke to each other behind fluttering hand fans.

My mother picked several needles out of my hair and sat me in the chair beside her. She turned back to the Duchess and started to speak, but the noblewoman raised her hand, and my mother fell silent. The Duchess smiled and winked at me. With the muffled clap of her gloved hands, Wadsworth pulled a lever and the whole gazebo whirled to life as gears began to turn and springs ticked in rhythm.

An automaton of a golden-maned lion, in a servant's suit, poured cups of tea from a pot and lowered them onto a series of silver swans' necks. The mechanical birds moved about on tracks in the floor serving tea to the ladies. The swans also carried small teacakes and sandwiches on golden trays perched on their backs.

The automatons were so much more elaborate than the one I'd seen in Paris de l'aire. Londaria was the most powerful of the aircities, and the hi-nobles were the richest too. I watched the ballet of mechanical servants in awe.

A servant walked up and handed the Duchess a note. She unfolded the parchment and without a single change to her expression, handed it back. "I'm afraid the Princess will be unable to join us this afternoon."

Many of the guests moaned, then a flurry of private and hushed conversations rippled through the gazebo. The woman next to me, with long feathers rising off her head, leaned over and whispered to my mother, "She's been seen less and less lately. Rumor is the Queen and her ministers won't let her."

My mother looked concerned, and her hand covered her heart. "Oh my, really. The demands of court. It's unfortunate she won't be coming."

"I know, and I even wore my best gown hoping to be noticed."

"Oh?" My mother said as she looked over the woman's dress. "It's lovely, Lady Goldwarbler."

"The Queen will be choosing the Princess' friends for the next year. I hope to be selected."

I piped up. "Why doesn't the Princess just keep her friends?" I'd been friends with the crew my whole life.

My mother put her hand on my leg, the international symbol that I needed to be quiet, but I didn't understand why. Nobles never made any sense.

The woman's face drained of joy, "You're too young to know. Years ago, someone close betrayed the royal family and killed the King and Queen. The King's sister became Queen and raised their daughter as her own."

"Whoa." That sounded like all the historical stories my tutor made me read. "Did they arrest the guy who betrayed them?"

"No." She leaned closer to me. "We're not even sure who it was."

"Was it the Nightraven?"

"The thief? I don't think so, but one never knows in these situations."

My mother gripped my leg a little tighter – the international symbol for enough.

The noble woman kissed the top of my head as I retracted. "Rumors say it was a dragonrider." The word ignited my insides. I wanted to know more about these people who ride dragons through the sky.

Of course. Everything made sense. Something that big and terrible explained why they still fight to this day. I wanted to hear more about the war and the Princess, but a man in black robes and funny hat entered the gazebo. He walked from one woman to the next, saying hello and running his hands creepily along their shoulders.

The Duchess smiled, but looked annoyed. "Lord High Chancellor Rycroft, to what do we owe this honor."

"I'm afraid with the Nightraven on the loose, I could not let the Princess join you ladies. I thought I would stop by to present my… sincerest apologies." He leaned back on his heels as he said the last part.

The Duchess said, "That was unnecessary, but we thank you for joining us. Unfortunately, this is a ladies' garden party. Men, even chancellors, are not allowed."

"But I see a young man among these ladies." He pointed to me with a slithering smile.

"As you said he is a young man, a boy, who should not stray far from his mother." The Duchess smiled and winked at me.

"I can't argue with that logic." He looked at me with beady black eyes and his voice curled up. "Enjoy yourself with these lovely ladies, Master… Greyvenhorn. Ah, yes the inspector's son." With a creepy crooked-smile, he watched everyone here, and my spine started wiggly-wobbling.

My mother warned me about men who were all handshakes and smiles. He probably could argue with that logic.

A voice broke the tension thickening in the garden. My father walked up in his usual stiff and rigid posture. "Pardon my intrusion ladies, do forgive me Duchess. Lord High Chancellor Rycroft, may I speak to you about the inspections?"

The Duchess' lips thinned and her brow scrunched up into deep lines.

The Lord High Chancellor rolled his eyes and I got the

feeling he didn't like my father. "Inspector Greyvenhorn, what is it I can do for *you*?"

My father motioned for the Lord High Chancellor to step away. "I still have not been granted access to the lower levels."

The chancellor didn't move. "Inspector, I told you we are renovating. I must ensure your safety."

"I would feel at ease if I could verify the numbers."

"I told you, those reports contained errors." The minster smiled, a well-practiced expression. I didn't feel his joy. Only tension. "I know." The Lord High Chancellor raised his finger. "Why don't you visit Skye Outpost. Check them off your list, and by the time you return we will be able to get you into the Main Airdrainium Processing Chamber."

"I suppose, but I need to inspect the secondary and back-up chambers in Londaria as well."

"Yes, yes, of course." The Lord High Chancellor raised his hand to the Duchess and folded them into his black robe. "Come, we shall discuss a timetable for your inspections."

My mother raised her head. I hadn't notice her keep it down, but now she watched my father and the Lord High Chancellor walking back toward the house. Her eyes narrowed, but the Duchess said, "Now that the men's drama has departed we can get back to my wonderful new dressmaker." Everyone applauded and my mother snapped back into the gazebo.

I wasn't certain what was going on, but then I didn't care anymore, my stomach grumbled just as the silver swans carried trays of food, stopping in front of each lady and me. Lunch!

# Chapter 8

I rushed up to my room to get out of this suit. I had only a few hours until the next boring hi-noble party. Before I could get my jacket off, a shadow whipped past the window. I ran over and saw an archangel soaring down the street.

His head darted back and forth as he scanned for someone. Behind him in the alleyway, I saw a figure dressed all in black with a strange mask. The figure clung to the shadows and disappeared. I searched until I found him further down, hidden in a doorway.

"The Nightraven!" I pressed against the glass to see as far down the street as possible. "I bet he's trying to avoid the archangel. I should follow them."

If I'd thought about what I said for more than two seconds, this would have sounded like a bad idea but I didn't. I ran off still in my suit.

I thought about telling the guards, but I didn't see any as I ran out the side of the house. I ran across the grounds and jumped over the outer stone wall. The archangel hovered at the end of the street I looked down the alley and saw a shadow dart behind a building.

The alley led toward the airdocks. I ran down the street

and rounded the corner. The archangel flew between the airships. I jumped on top of some crates and searched for the Nightraven. A figure darted out from behind several stacked barrels and crept toward a dirigible. I looked up and saw the Caledonia, my airship. The Nightraven was stealing the dresses!

I had to warn the crew. There should be a few people still onboard.

I ran to the gangplank and rushed onto the Caledonia. "Captain! Rohl! Anyone?"

I didn't hear any responses. That didn't mean they weren't onboard just not nearby. I ran toward the portside. There, I saw the Nightraven climbing up the steam-pipes wrapped around the outside. He hopped onto the catwalk's metal grating, and didn't make a sound. He crept toward the outer hatch. I bet he'd used the door to gain entry to the Caledonia unnoticed. If I got there first, maybe he'd run away.

The thought that he might attack me made it hard to take another step, but this was my home. I couldn't let the Nightraven break in. I rushed to the middle of the ship.

I reached the outer hatch and heard someone shifting on the deck plating on the other side. It had to be the Nightraven.

What do I do? I thought about my options. I could rush out and attack, but I wasn't a warrior. I pressed my back against the door in some vain attempt to keep it closed, but if the Nightraven had any strength, he'd push right past me. I needed to stop him, capture him. Yeah right, I wish. I'm twelve. The Nightraven evaded archangels. And a kid was going to stop him. I paused.

Dogger was good at fighting, and he liked to surprise people with his haymaker. If I surprised the Nightraven maybe he'd run. I looked around for a weapon. Anything that would make me look intimidating.

I saw two links of the anchor chain. Each one was as big as my head and made of iron. I grabbed it by one end and pulled with all my might. I pushed open the hatch with a mighty barbaric yawp and whipped the chain-links forward. I saw my mother standing on the deck, she threw up her arms in surprise. I tried to stop the chain but it was too heavy. It slammed down on the deck plating making a clank that echoed across the docks.

"Mom?"

"Anderax, what are you doing here?"

I dropped the chain. "Why are you here?"

An archangel soared up from below. "Halt in the name of the crown and clergy."

I froze and my mother pulled me against her. "What seems to be the trouble?"

"I seek a thief last seen in this area."

"Well we've been on this ship for a couple of hours, I haven't seen anyone."

I looked up at my mother. We hadn't been here that long. But I didn't say anything, the milky, haunting eyes of the archangel made me shudder.

"Good evening, madam." With a nod of his head the archangel darted over the next airship and disappeared.

I turned to my mom, but before I could speak she rushed me inside the Caledonia. "What are you doing out of the Duke's house young man?"

Every question I had slipped away on the wind, and I

stammered to find an answer. I needed something good, or I wouldn't be leaving my room for days. "I was following you."

She froze, but then leaned back on her heel and eyed me. "Are you sure?"

My shoulders slumped. "No. I just said that so I wouldn't get in trouble. I was following the Nightraven."

A blank stare crossed her face. It meant she was thinking, hard. I jumped as I remembered seeing the Nightraven on our dock. I bolted from her arms and ran for the docking clamp.

"I saw the Nightraven over this way. Maybe he's still there. That's why the archangel was nearby."

"Anderax I don't want you chasing the Nightraven."

I didn't listen. The last thing I wanted to do was stop. Maybe I was part cat, because curiosity's grasp was unbreakable. I rushed out the hatch where the huge iron arm clamped down on the airship. Darting from one side to the other I checked for the Nightraven but didn't see anything. With airships docked all around, he could have gone anywhere.

"Oh, well. He's probably slipped away when the archangel arrived."

The hatch blew open and my mother rushed out. She snatched me by the arm and dragged me back inside. "Anderax, you will listen to me. These are dangerous times and we must be careful. Now I do not want you to speak of this to your father or anyone within the Duke's house. Is that understood?"

"Okay."

"Anderax, I'm serious. This is important."

"If my father finds out I was chasing an archangel he'll be really angry. Right?"

"Your father loves you. He's only concerned about you. He thinks you have too much of me in you."

"I think that's a good thing."

"Me too." She kissed my forehead. "No, we can't tell anybody because… well, to help your father."

"Oh. I won't tell anyone. Promise."

She wiped a tear from her cheek and we walked down the Caledonia's gangplank. I didn't understand what made her so sad. I really hoped it wasn't me.

# Chapter 9

A few hours passed, bringing another suit jacket and another boring dinner. Did these nobles do anything but eat? I brushed off my sleeve and joined my parents in the hall.

My mother remained in her robe and dressing gown, and coughed loudly. She held her arm out as I approached. "Don't get too close, I think I've come down with something." She sniffled and dabbed her nose with a handkerchief.

I stayed back, but she hadn't been like this an hour ago. Must be a fast-moving bug, and if so, I didn't want to get it. I was bored enough. Days stuck in bed – I might not survive.

My father took me by the shoulder and said to my mother, "I'm sorry you can't attend dinner. I hear the Princess will be there."

"Oh no, that is truly tragic news. I missed her at lunch today as well." My mother covered face with her handkerchief as if about to sneeze.

"I can't get sick right now." My father rushed me down the hall. "I have a schedule."

He led me to the dining hall where once again I faced the long thin table with flower centerpieces and golden plates. Only this time, I didn't have my mother to sit beside. My father put me in a chair next to a tall grandpa like man. Lord Crane, as he introduced himself, owned a bank. The strong scent of powder and perfume assaulted my nose. If I survived tonight it would be a miracle.

I watched each noble at the table. Every conversation mentioned the Nightraven, and everyone had a different opinion on who he might be. Lord Crane, leaned over to a woman beside him, the one with blue streaks in her hair. "What I want to know… what is this Nightraven doing in Londaria?"

Lady Goldwarbler, who had feathers rising two feet off her hat said, "The Nightraven struck LuftBerlin when I was there. He wore a grand black cape, and a giant, feathery mask with a *looong* beak."

Another woman in blue polka-dots, Lady Starling, gasped and covered her face with a fan. "Oh my, how did you survive?"

Feathers bobbed back and forth as Lady Goldwarbler pecked at her plate. "We almost died."

I didn't believe them. Rohl always said shifty eyes were the sign of a liar, and not a single person actually made eye contact as they talked.

Lord Littleton, a man in a curly wig across the table from me, laughed and said, "He most certainly did not, I faced the demon in Paris d'Laire. A creature of feather and claws."

Lady Goldwarbler gasped, "How dare you call me a liar. He wore a feathery mask and has diamonds on the tips of his cape to cut glass windows."

Lord Hawfinch shook his head, the large curls of his long wig bounced about his shoulders. "Madam, you are mistaken, he is half-bird.

Tension rose until it lay thick over the table like a fog. I had to say something, they're just telling lies to impress each other. In my best gentlemanly voice and tone, just as my mother taught me, I said, "Perhaps it was dark when you both saw him. I witnessed the Nightraven the other night. He didn't have feathers, but clothes black as night. He wore a mask, but of simple leather. I didn't see a long beak."

"What a foolish child." Lord Hawfinch said.

"As if a child could understand such things." Lady Goldwarbler bobbed her head as she chuckled. The rest of the hi-nobles laughed and the tension disappeared.

Heat rose on the back of my neck, but an icy chill rippled through me as soldiers marched in a column through one of the doors. Excitement rippled through the rest of the guests.

I thought we might be arrested, but the soldiers remained in formation. A woman in a shimmering gown stepped through the doors, and glided across the room with effortless grace. Everyone leap to their feet, and bowed their heads. I knew I should too, and I stood, but I couldn't lower my head. I had to see.

Blonde hair cascaded in thick locks down the sides of her face, and she wore a silver crown studded with rubies. Her beauty made me smile, but she had such a familiar face. As she approached everyone turned away, as if to look on her directly was wrong. However, as she passed them, they would sneak glances. Especially her dress. I didn't look away and we locked eyes for a brief moment. She smiled, and I instantly recognized my mother. But why?

The more I stared the more differences I saw, beside the hair. The Princess looked identical to my mother, except in the eyes. The Princess had a sad softness to her eyes that my mother didn't have. I wanted to ask why, but she remained ringed by guards.

The Duke welcomed the Princess to the table and gave up his seat.

I couldn't stop staring, If my mother were here, she'd spin my head around. She wasn't here though, and if she were, I'd just stare at her and compare. I whipped around expecting my father to be staring too, but he wasn't. He didn't even notice her. His head remained bowed like the others. He wore glasses, but he had a keen eye that could spot the minor movements of an aircity. What was going on? Why wasn't the Duchess telling the Princess about her identical twin the dress maker?

Even when the hi-nobles did speak, they didn't look directly at the Princess. The conversation changed too. No one mentioned the Nightraven. Most talked about the pleasant weather.

Through the first three courses of dinner, I couldn't stop glancing at the Princess. The blonde hair made me doubt myself, but she had the same dimples. I ran my fingers across my the very same dimples on my face. If it weren't for the hair, I would swear she was my mother.

Confused, I dug my fork into the next course, but it just twirled in my hands as I thought about why my mother wasn't here.

54

# Chapter 10

After dinner, I followed my father back to our rooms. I wanted to ask about the Princess, but he kept mumbling to himself about the inspections. "I do hope the Duke can get me in the lower levels tomorrow, or I'll be late checking on Skye Outpost."

"What's down there?"

My father snapped a look at me surprised by my voice. "Where?"

"The lower levels. They sound fun, more interesting than nobles eating."

He pulled away and shook his head. "You don't need to concern yourself with the lower levels."

*   *   *

The crash of thunder and the flash of lightning woke me in the morning. My father opened the door, "Be ready to depart this afternoon. We'll be leaving on the Caledonia for a day or two."

"You bet!" Getting away from the hi-nobles for a few days sounded like a great idea.

"I have to make several inspections, but there are storms between here and Skye Outpost so we need to leave before the worst of it."

"I'll be ready."

"Dress warm. The wind is strong at Skye Outpost." My father closed the door and I rushed to get ready. I had to sit around forever after that. My father didn't return from the lower level inspections until almost nightfall.

My mother poked her head into my room, "Your father is back so get everything you need to visit the outpost."

"How long will it take to get there?"

"Not too long you'll only be gone a couple of days."

"Aren't you coming?"

"I have to finish the Duchess' dress."

"Oh." I turned back to the window streaked with rivers of rain.

"Don't worry. Rohl and the rest of the boys will keep you entertained."

"Can I ask you something, about dinner last night?"

"Of course, but remember it for when you get back. We have to get you on the Caledonia."

I nodded. Then grabbed my bag and ran out with my mother. "The best part… I don't have to wear a tie!"

My father and I rushed through the rain drops and boarded the Caledonia. We turned to wave goodbye to my mother who waved frantically from underneath an awning. She dabbed her eyes with a handkerchief. Seeing her sad made me sad. I didn't want to leave her, but I needed to get away from the hi-nobles, or the boredom would turn me into a statue. A few days on the Caledonia, tucked up in my steam-tree fort, would make me feel like me again.

I waved one last time. My father walked up to the captain, "Head for Skye Outpost, Captain Campbell. I'll be there a few days to inspect their equipment. Then we return to Londaria."

The captain nodded. "At once, sir. All is ready. As for the storm, sir, I can go around at the cost of a day, or we can risk going through."

"Best we go around then, for safety."

"Very good, sir."

"Captain, we depart at your earliest convenience. I will be in my office. Anderax is joining us, but my wife must remain behind to finish the Duchess' new gown."

"Very well, sir. The crew will make certain the lad doesn't get into too much trouble." My father and the captain glanced my way. I shrugged and they continued talking.

Spinning back toward the gangplank, I looked for my mother, to wave at her one more time. I scanned the docks but didn't see her.

Rohl came up behind me and nudged my shoulder. "It will be good to be in the sky again. Aeronauts were meant to fly." As he and I walked off, Rohl asked, "Did you see anything extraordinary in the city?"

"No, nothing fun. Boring noble stuff. Everyone just sits around in fancy clothes, eating."

"That sounds like fun to me." Rohl laughed and his large belly shook. "I bet they had prime rib and gravy." He rubbed his tummy and bit his lip as he stared off at the dock. I shook my head and kept walking along the catwalk. Rohl rushed to catch up. "We'll have fun for the next few days then."

"Sounds good." I high-fived him and ran off. I knew he wanted me to go to my room, to stay inside where it was safe, but that wasn't what I wanted. Running along the catwalk, I climbed the steam pipes to my platform. Pulling the gearkey from my pocket, I fit it into place. With a quarter rotation to the right, I raised the hatch, and slipped into my steamtree fort. I dropped into my hammock and let out a deep breath. I was home. No more stiff suits. No more not-being-able-to-touch-anything, and definitely no more hi-nobles.

Above me were boards and metal planks creating the roof, not gold and curly decorations. I scooped up a glider from the floor underneath me, and made it dive and bank in an aerial dogfight. Tilting the flaps on the wings down and tilting one more than the other, I threw the glider. It started down toward the floor but then swooped up and banked back returning to me like a boomerang.

Twice more I threw the glider, and it followed the same path back to me. The Caledonia lurched and we departed from Londaria. Through the portholes, the city drifted off on the clouds.

I bent the flaps on the wings so they were all the way up and it looped in air a couple of times before sliding across the floor. Rolling over, I stared at a map I'd pinned to a cork wall. Rohl put an old map of the world on it, and all last year we placed a pin in every location we visited. I traced our flight path in red string my mother gave me. We'd been to every European aircity, bounced from one side of the Mediterranean Sea to the other a dozen times. We'd seen the tallest mountains in the east, and been as far south as the great desert where it could be too hot to fly.

Once the raging storm winds ended, I rolled out of the hammock. Wrapping the lifeline around my waist, I secured the buckle. The other end held a brass hook that latched onto the railing. I pulled down on a cord hanging by the back wall. A beam in the ceiling lowered and formed stairs. I climbed out onto the deck and the wind whipped around me. I hooked my lifeline to the railing and walked toward the edge of the rain-soaked sundeck.

I scanned the skies for any signs of dragons. I didn't know what exactly to look for, but I knew a few things. They were big. They flew. They roared.

I gripped the railing, thinking of the roar I'd heard a few days ago. Yanking my goggles up over my eyes I smiled. The sun's warmth kept the chilly, rain-soaked wind from freezing me to the core. Londaria hung in the distance, surrounded by storm clouds that stretched to the horizon. In front of the storm, the clouds were broken up enough to see over the port side. Thousands of feet below, deep blue water tipped with white lay in every direction.

"The ocean, we're over the ocean!"

Sunlight dance on the surface, and I grabbed my telescope for a better view. The surface churned in constant motion. I didn't think anything could exist in such a strange environment, but then several dark shapes burst out of the surface with their huge mouths opened in unison. They sprayed jets of water in the air, rolled and slipped back under the surface. "Whales, real whales!"

I watched them until we'd travel too far and couldn't see them above the surface. If there were creatures that big in the water, why couldn't there be huge creatures in the sky. I looked out over the horizon to see if I could find any sign of dragons, but nothing. The endless blue above was bigger than anything I'd ever seen. It arched across the horizon, stretching in every direction. I'd traveled through only a small part, but had never heard of an edge of the sky.

The next morning, Rohl stepped out on the catwalk. He cupped his hands around his mouth, "Your father wishes you to join him on the bridge of the airship."

I raised my thumb and rushed inside my steamtree fort. I closed the door and popped down through the hatch. High-fiving Rohl as I ran by. I rushed through the Caledonia. Dropping down the stairs two at a time.

The lowest deck of the airship led to the gondola attached to the bottom, where the captain and crew piloted the Caledonia. I opened the hatch and stepped inside the long, narrow room. Brisco, the pilot, sat at the front. Behind him, the captain had chair but he usually stood. The engineer's station was back by me, with the map table between him and the captain.

My father stood with the Captain at the map table. They looked up and called me over. "Anderax," my father said pushing his glasses up on his nose. "I thought you might like this. The captain is searching for Skye Outpost which is on our current heading." He pulled his pocket watch from his vest pocket. He flipped open the silver watch on a long chain. "In ten minutes we should be arriving."

The captain pointed to a small x marked on the map. "The outpost should be right here."

"I thought you might want to see our arrival."

"Sounds interesting." I walked up to the window. "I was watching whales in the ocean."

"Ah yes." My father said, but he was reading through several papers and I don't think he really heard me.

The captain watched the sky. Turning all the way around he scanned the clouds as if looking for something. The pilot, Brisco, called me over.

"Best seat in the Caledonia." Brisco, who wore a white scarf around his dark-skinned neck, tugged on his shaded-lens goggles. "Three hundred and sixty degrees of sky."

"Makes me feel like I'm flying."

"Exactly. Here," Brisco slid back his chair, which sat in a slot on the floor, allowing him to get in out but still be close to all the controls. The chair even had a lever that locked it in place. "Stand here and you can pilot the Caledonia."

"Excellent!" I stepped in front of Brisco, but he kept one hand on the yoke.

The wooden and brass wheel was as wide as my shoulders, and I wrapped my finders around the outer ring. Spokes led to a central point attached to a gimble, allowing it to turn, as well as moving forward and back, and side to side. I held firm, fearing if I made the wrong move we'd crash into the outpost.

"Keep her steady. Look at your compass to make sure you're heading in the right direction. Then find a point in the distance and fly to it. Not a cloud, though, they move."

"Wow, but there is nothing on the horizon."

"You need to feel the map… our longitude and latitude. Eventually you'll see them as if they were drawn in the sky."

"Really?"

"Look hard you might see them."

I stared out the window, straining my eyes. Brisco flipped a switch on the panel and lines formed on the glass. Thin ink lines crossed on the glass. The pencil line that marked our current path rose right up through the center of the window. "I can see it." I moved, and my shadow blocked part of the map. Spinning on my heel, I found a bright light hanging from the ceiling, blinding me.

Brisco and the crew laughed as I squinted. Moving out of the light, I saw a projector above the map table. My father pointed at something on the map as his finger moved on the window.

"Hey, those are the lines from the map."

"They are." Brisco calmed down and pointed into the sky. "Come on, we have our last turn coming up. Time to focus."

Grabbing the wheel once again, I looked up at the pencil line and saw it turn to the right.

The captain called out in a booming voice, "Course correction, bearing thirty degrees starboard. All ahead full."

Brisco said, "Aye, aye, captain." He nudged my side, "All right, turn the wheel slowly, until you see this compass hit the 30-degree mark.

"Aye, aye, pilot." Turning the wheel caused the Caledonia to bank. The numbers ticked by one by one, until it approached the big thirty on the compass.

"There you go. Bring the wheel back to center and ease out of the turn."

"I did it!" I looked to see if my father was watching but he was still going over his papers. However, Captain Campbell's beaming smile was a pretty good substitute.

"Excellent work, Master Grayvenhorn," the captain nodded and then turned as a pneumatic tube shot out of the ceiling and slid through the tube along the wall. A crewman retrieved the note and handed it to the captain. "Skye Outpost directly ahead."

Off in the distance, I saw a dot. A dark speck bobbing above the clouds. Skye Outpost.

# Chapter 11

Never had I seen an aircity dance so wildly atop the clouds. The Caledonia bobbed along in the strong stormy winds. The aircity must be affected as well.

I kept expecting the city to grow bigger, but as we approached the docks I could still see both sides. Stone and metal rose up in several spires that spun on a central axis that looked like a standing stone.

"See her dancing with the clouds?" Brisco asked. "The wind'll push her twenty miles in any direction."

"Wow. That's far." I looked out the window to broken lands and churning seas below. "Wobblesmocking, definitely wobblesmocking out there."

"You got that right."

"Bring us about, match their rotational speed, and prepare for docking." The captain's booming voice behind me made me jump.

Pilot turned the wheel and adjusted the throttle levers, "Aye, aye."

The Caledonia slipped closer to the aircity. The large iron docking clamp extended out, and pilot slipped the airship into the pocket. The clamp secured onto the hull and gently drew us the last few feet to the airdocks.

The captain turned to his engineer. "Send word to Rohl to tie us down tight."

The engineer scribbled a note and sent it off through one of the pneumatic tubes.

My father tapped me on the shoulder. "We should prepare for our arrival ceremony. I want you dressed in a nice suit and standing at the gangplank in five minutes."

Three minutes later I was standing at the gangplank waiting for my father. It would have taken all five, but I didn't wear a tie and hoped no one would notice.

My father walked up dressed in the same black suit with a long tailcoat, that he'd worn every day of his life. If I hadn't seen the closet full of black suits, I would have sworn he only owned one suit. I wore grey. I didn't have many colors, men only had a few options.

My father's joyful expression quickly faded as his eyes narrowed on my neck. "Where is you tie?"

"I didn't think I needed one, and they're tight."

"He scoffed. A proper gentleman needs to be dressed as such. A proper suit comes with a proper tie. Captain, may I borrow your tie?"

Standing at the door, the captain nodded, and loosened the thin black tie from his neck. He handed it to my father who slipped the tie over my head. The ends hung down past the bottom of my jacket. My father tucked them in my shirt, then closed my jacket and buttoned it.

"There, now you look like a proper gentleman."

"Why are we here?"

"Their airdrainium chamber is having trouble. Enough to pull me away from inspections in Londaria."

The captain opened the door, and my father stood up. He tugged his jacket into place, and we walked down the gangplank. Three men in suits with tartan sashes over their right shoulders stood on the airdocks. The one in the center had dark hair and a large broach pin over his heart. With serious expressions on everyone's faces, I knew I shouldn't say a word, or fidget too much.

When we stepped onto the aircity, the whole complex wobbled. I held out my hands to steady myself. Airships could be tossed about by turbulence, but aircities didn't have that problem. I'd never had so much trouble standing in one place.

My father grabbed a railing and said, "What mixture are you using? Take me to the airdrainium chamber immediately."

The man on the left, marked with fiery red hair, said, "Do not worry, inspector. It's only the wind. Skye Outpost, moves about quite a bit."

He wasn't kidding. The wind whipped around me, pressing my clothes against me. I'd been to some of the windiest aircities in the western skies, but nothing like this place. My hair hadn't stopped moving since we stepped off the airship, and the guy with long red locks looked like his head was on fire.

"Inspector Grayvenhorn," The man with the broach said, "Name's Blacktern, tis a pleasure to host yah. A bit late, aren't we?"

"Do forgive us. A delay in Londaria that could not be avoided." My father stood straight and stiff as a board, but I was bobbing and weaving trying to stay on my feet.

The man with red hair said, "Ready to begin your tour, unless you need more time."

My father nodded. He adjusted his hat, a thin brimmed bowler, and pressed it further down on his head. The three men motioned for us to follow and we walked across the metal grating of the airdock. Scanning the outpost, I saw two young people in the distance. I wanted to run after them as they disappeared behind a building. My father pushed me on as, Blacktern signaled with his hand. A man staring down at us through slots in the wall, pulled a lever, and a huge iron arm lifted up, taking the main door with it.

As we walked inside, the slots slammed shut, and the arm slid the door back into place. The wind still howled and moaned through the metal corridors, as we entered the central core of the outpost. Looking up, metal plating and catwalks stretched up to the top. Parts of each floor were closed off for rooms, but the rest remained open. Skye Outpost resembled a tower more than a flat top like the other aircities I'd visited.

We stepped into a large metal cage and the red-haired man closed the gate behind us. Pulleys and gears sang as the ungreased metal began to move. Slowly, the elevator lowered us down through the central shaft of the outpost. I pressed myself against the metal cage letting my fingers grip the diamond-shaped openings.

Looking up, I watched as we fell away from the sunlight. Shifting my eyes down, flickering light from gas-lamp sconces on the walls lit the shaft. We passed huge gears and sprockets rotating slowly, and I realized the entire outpost was a giant machine, twisting and moving in some giant process.

I didn't know what for. Keeping the outpost in the sky, or something crazier. I leaned back, my fingers stilling gripping the cage. "What does this outpost do?"

My father smiled, adjusted his glasses, and looked like he was about to break into a huge lecture. "Well, Skye Outpost is an airdrainium processing center. They also harness wind, water, and lightning to be shipped to the other aircities."

He took a deep breath and continued on about how wind was pushed up through the outpost while, water was processed using gravity and passed to tanks underneath. I, however, stopped listening, and stared at the other people in this elevator. As my father talked, the three men leading us gave each other shifting glances. When the cage lurched, their eyes bulged, and rolled in some kind of conversation. My father didn't notice, he was pointing out one of the large coil springs.

The cage settled in a slot on the bottom floor. The red headed man opened the cage and we all stepped out. A chugging noise mixed with the loud bangs, whirling wind, and the hum of machinery to create a symphony of sound so loud, I couldn't hear my own thoughts anymore. I covered my ears with my hands but it did little to drown out the noise. The three men motioned for us to follow and my father pushed me along, keeping me in front of him.

We passed through several hatches. Heavy metal doors each latched in all four corners with a wheel in the center. After passing through each one, they would lock the hatch behind us before moving on to next.

I stared to feel trapped like beans in a can, but then we stepped into a circular hallway with a large door. Two of the men, opened the door, while Mr. Blacktern turned to my father, "Excellent, you will be able to see all is in order and hopefully we can have you back in Londaria by morning."

My father nodded, and said, "The inspection will take as long as it takes. I can go no faster than the thirty-six checkpoints allow."

"Of course, and anything you need will be provided. We appreciate you being able to stop by. Shame you had to be delayed or this might already be over. We have much work awaiting us."

"I assure you I will not impede your operations. Unless I find a glaring oversight."

The two men went silent as the large metal door swung out on a thick pin. It took both men to move the door, and they slid an iron bar out from the wall to hold it open. We stepped through into a large round chamber. A huge machine with tubes leading to large cylindrical tanks filled the center of the room. On the front of the machine sat a square door about two feet wide.

"Here she is," Blacktern said. "Skye Outpost's Airdrainium Processor."

"You've still got one of the old T5s." My father's eyes lit up. "I haven't seen one of these since we installed the new T9 in OlympusPeak."

The man with red hair said, "We make do with what we have."

Blacktern looked at me and extended his hands toward the machine. "Impressive isn't it."

"It's big." I stood next to a gear as tall as my shoulders. "Kind of… clunky.

My father spun around. "It's one hundred and fifty years old. Well, refurbished and improved on."

"Oh." Some parts had rusted making it easy to believe a century had past. "Looks old."

"Reliable. You see Anderax, this is the airdrainium processor. It collects the gases released when the ore comes in contact with water. There is a complex process I'm not going to go through now, but your tutor will, one day. Then those gases are pumped through the city keeping us aloft."

"Creating the clouds all aircities sit on."

"Correct." My father turned back to the machine, studying it with his complete attention.

The metal plating on the floor under the machine held deep scratches. Marks went in every direction with several parallel to each other. Some had darkened with dirt, meaning they were older, but other scratches were so new that the shiny metal still gleamed in the groove.

A sweet but irritating smell filled the air, and I longed for the clear air of blue skies. I coughed, and my father said, "The air's not that bad, but it should be thicker in here."

I didn't know what he meant, but I couldn't stop staring at the floor, as the others walked around the machine. I found four huge iron semi-circles sticking out of the floor two on one side of the room, and two on the other. I wondered what they were for, and what the deep scratch marks on them could mean.

My father glanced at Blacktern as he walked over to a wall of dials. "You're running the airdrainium mixture too thin. I noticed the wobble as we approached the outpost." After studying some of the gauges, he twisted several valves.

"There, that should stabilize the platform."

Quick glances darted between the three men, but rather than happy or relieved faces, tension quivered their lips, and stiffened their muscles. My father didn't notice. His head was in the machine. The dark-haired man with the broach looked at me, nudged the other two men with his elbows, and their stoic faces returned.

My father rolled up his sleeve and reached into a small opening in the big machine. I couldn't see what, but he appeared to be fiddling with something. He reached in even further, all the way to the shoulder of his jacket. "You're dangerously low on your airdrainium." He pulled his arm out, rolled down his sleeve, and turned around. "This needs to be replenished, immediately."

"Inspector, you are here to check the machines. Keep yer other thoughts to yourself." The man with the broach said. "We've got a… another shipment coming. I'm sure after you've departed, they'll arrive." He chuckled, and the men joined in.

My skin crawled with each cackle. However, my father didn't even flinch at their words. He was already inspecting the air-lines, thick tubes covered in thick canvas and a thin metal coil. With a large jeweler's loop connected to a metal band so it could fit around the brim of his hat, my father studied every inch of hose.

Shifting on their feet, and checking their pocket watches, the three men watched my father's every move.

My father took off the loop. He folded it up, pulled the leather case from his pocket and placed it inside. As he slipped it back in his pocket, he turned to me. "Are we ready to sign off on this airdrainium processor, junior inspector."

I died. Not really, but I did want to melt through the gaps in the floor and disappear. Junior Inspector was his nickname for me when I was younger, like five. *I'm way past the name, but he insists on calling me that. Rohl's told me how I used to follow him around with a magnifying glass. But I didn't want to be an inspector. I wanted to be... I'm not sure yet.* However, all I said was, "Looks good to me."

My father walked over to the men. "Excellent, let us move on to the Collector Coils and continue this inspection."

I snapped my head up, looking at my father. "Do I have to go? I could walk around the promenade or head back to the Caledonia."

"The coils are fascinating. They can be over a hundred feet long."

"You showed me the ones in LuftBerlin. I should get to my homework." I didn't want to work on homework. I wanted to find those kids again. They were probably having fun. They might even have the cure for my boredom.

"I suppose your studies are important. When we've returned to the main deck, you can head back to the Caledonia." He grabbed my shoulder and together we walked out with the three men following behind us.

The man with the broach nodded to the third man, whose mustache curled out to waxed tips. The man darted off as we turned a corner. I wonder where he could be going, but my father pushed me on. The two men led us back to the main deck. When we could see the Caledonia perched on the airdocks, my father let me go.

I ran to the airship. My hand grabbed the railing of the

gangplank, but as I stepped on two dark shapes zipped across the edge of my vision. I turned my head, but whatever I'd seen had vanished. Darting along the catwalks, I went to find the pair. When I reached a giant set of pistons rising and falling through each revolution, two people in short blue coats darted behind a generator. I rounded the corner to follow, and sparks showered down on me. The metal walkway ended in a wall. No doors. Nowhere to escape. Nowhere to run.

I spun on my heel and even looked up, but nothing.

"I saw you!" I yelled into the howling wind. Through all the noise, the clank of a boot on metal planking rang clear like a bell. I ran back around the corner. A boy with short brown hair stood on the catwalk, adjusting the stuffed-leather satchel over his shoulder. He pointed at me, and a girl with long red hair pulled herself over the railing and hopped onto the catwalk. They looked my age, but instead of being dressed as aircity mechanics, they wore short blue jackets and tight brown pants. I'd never seen such form-fitting clothes. I didn't know what to say, but I had to say something… "Hi."

The girl said, "Hi."

"I'm bored," popped right of my mouth.

"What?" The girl's brow scrunched up. "You're bored."

"Very. What are you guys doing?"

"We have to go." The boy said.

Both their heads snapped back and forth as if expecting more people to show up. *Were they in an area they weren't supposed to be?* I wanted to ask, but really, I wanted them to stay.

"Wait…" I said, and they froze.

A loud grinding sound erupted from within the outpost

and the whole structure shuttered. My eyes grew, but my stomach dropped. The outpost lurched and slipped several feet. Tilting to one side, the entire structure started toppling over. I wrapped my arm around the railing to keep from flying away.

The other two fell and slid along the metal planking. I reached out and grabbed hold of the girl's jacket as she passed. She snatched the boy by the arm. "Ahhh," I groaned as my elbow strained around the railing. Swinging them toward the railing, the girl snagged a bar of her own. She pushed the boy onto rail and he clung to it tightly.

"My father once told me if an airship ever lists, to get to a wall. Same must be true for an aircity." I climbed the railing like a ladder, and they followed. We shimmied along until we reached a wall of the outpost. With one foot on the floor and one foot on the wall, we were finally able to stand… sort of.

"Thank you, for the help," the boy said.

"Yes. Thank you." The girl added.

"We should keep moving," I said. "We don't know how much further the outpost will lean."

"Our rides will be worried about us." The girl said.

"Yeah," I glanced over my shoulder toward the airdocks. "I need to get to my airship."

They looked at me, and I cocked my head. Something was odd about these two. The boy checked around the corner. He pulled the strap of the leather satchel over his head and handed it to the girl. She slung it over her head and slipped her arm through. Settling the bag on her hip, she turned to me. "Thanks again."

The boy stepped to the edge. "Time to go. Guards are gone."

"Guards, who are you guys?" I asked.

They glanced at each other and smiled. The boy jumped off, landed on a catwalk, and slid down it like a slide.

"What are your names?" I asked the girl.

"We don't really do names."

"Then what do I call you?"

"Dragonrider." She said, then she too jumped onto the catwalk and slid away. I ran and looked around the wall. She and the boy raced to the edge of the outpost and sprang into the clouds with a giant leap. I reached out in disbelief, as if my arm would grow and catch them both. They tumbled into clouds and stopped. Both knelt on a cloud. Shiny red-leathery scales whipped through the puffy white wall before disappearing back into the mist.

"Dragon!" I squinted, staring into the clouds hoping to see more.

A dark shape filled the clouds. The mist kept it hidden, but a large eye the size of a dinner plate emerged in front of me. Blue leathery scales enveloped the eye, and the large slit widened as it stared right through me.

Another dragon. This one was bigger, much bigger than the one I'd seen a moment ago.

Waves of awe washed over me mixed with swirling fear. As terror zapped my energy confidence swelled within me. Instead of my legs wobbling, I locked in my stance like a statue. Staring at this creature, I found a soft soul lay within the eye. For me, I was seeing a depth in the swirling colors of the eye. A starry sky on the darkest of nights. I didn't see evil, or a mindless beast, but intelligence. An eye watching me, as much as I studied it. The creature banked off, whipping up the clouds in its wake.

The outpost lurched and slipped several feet again. I grabbed the railing, but unless I wanted to see the ground the hard way, I had to leave too. I'd never seen an aircity turn on its side, and what if it flipped over? The wind whipped ever faster against my face. The clouds rushed away, and my heart sunk… we were falling.

I climbed the railing trying to get to the airdock. When I reached a building, I ran along the wall to where the Caledonia had been docked. Nothing sat in the mooring clamps. They had gotten away, but I was stuck. Searching to the left, up, down, and to the right, I looked for the Caledonia but didn't see them. I tried to wave my arms at an airskiff hovering above me, but they flew away from the outpost.

My mother always said, not listening would get me in trouble and she was right. If I'd gotten on the Caledonia, I'd be fine. But I didn't.

A shadow crept over me. I looked up. Blocking out the sun was the Caledonia. I jumped up, reaching out with my arms, but a hundred feet or more remained.

My father, the captain, Dogger, and Rohl, stood on one of the airship's catwalks. They all talked over each other as they pointed at me. The outpost lurched again, and I slid along the wall. Everyone above me panicked, but I used a gutter to catch myself, and popped back on my feet.

Dogger grabbed a spooler, a long spear gun with a huge coil of rope. He anchored it to the railing and fired. A grappling hook sailed toward me, and slammed into the wall.

Unable to pierce the thick metal walls it scraped away from me toward the far edge. In a moment, my only chance of getting off would slip away from me. Pushing with every ounce of strength in my muscles, I ran toward the line. The grappler fell off the side, I leapt off, and snatched it in the air. Gripping the rope tight, I wrapped my leg around. Rohl and Dogger pulled me up. Once again, I searched the clouds to find the dragons, but they had vanished along with the two riders.

# Chapter 12

Dogger pulled me over the railing and ruffled my hair after checking for injuries. My father pushed past him, and squeezed me tight. "Are you okay? I was so worried when you weren't on the ship." He pulled back from me and knelt down.

"I'm fine. No worse than the Caledonia in a bad storm."

"Let's not tell your mother about this."

I nodded. She would be really worried.

Ear-splitting grinding, knocking, and groaning sounds echoed up from below. Blasts of air shot up and pushed the Caledonia higher into the sky. I grabbed hold of the metal underneath the wooden railing. Everyone looked down. The bottom of Skye Outpost swung underneath the top like pendulum. I'd never seen an aircity move so violently.

The outpost fell, plunging through the clouds straight down toward the ground. Everything went silent, leaving only the soft hum of the Caledonia.

I gasped and pulled myself against the railing. Never would I have imagined seeing an aircity plummet from the sky. Such things didn't happen. My father made certain things like that didn't happen. I looked up at him. Pain filled his eyes, but he didn't take his eyes off the structure. I glanced at the rest of the crew. All had the same stunned expression as my father. I stared back down at the outpost. Gliders and parachute pods popped off as it fell and trailed behind it in a shower of silk. The outpost slammed into the water, sending a column of churned up ocean into the sky. Waves raced out in every direction.

My eyes couldn't pull away from the tangled-heap of torn metal half-submerged in water. Through the huge hole left in the clouds, I saw the blue waters of the ocean lapping against the structure. I couldn't remember the last time so much below was visible. Waves slammed against the rocky shoreline, as the land stretched out into the waters like fingers.

Several airships descended to collect the parachute pods drifting down. My father put his hands on my shoulders and turned to the captain. "Return to Londaria at once. I must tell the Lord High Chancellor." He pulled me from the railing, and we stepped inside. We traveled up the stairs to our apartment as the captain and others went to bridge.

I stopped and glanced over my shoulder, "Thanks, Dogger. Great shot."

He shot me with a finger-gun, and continued on toward the engine room.

My father and I entered our living room, and I asked, "What happened to the outpost?"

"They either didn't have enough airdrainium, or they used fake ore."

"Fake airdrainium?"

He pulled off his gloves and grabbed a small gray stone from one of his vest's pockets. "I'll have to do some calculations, and find out what this is." He walked into his office examining the stone.

The Caledonia circled the large hole in the clouds, moving off with the wind. I stared at the sea and shore below. All I saw was dark rock and green grass. No trees. We headed south, but I couldn't take my eyes off the crashed aircity. Soon clouds covered the world, and I lost the dream of seeing the trees below.

I kept my forehead pressed against the cool glass. I didn't know what to think anymore. Aircities hung in the sky for two hundred years, and in all that time not a single one even slipped more than a few inches. My father dedicated his life to keeping them in the sky. Now I'd seen one fall. *What could happen next?*

The Caledonia shuddered. Turbulence. We ran into it all the time, and I'd never thought about the choppy air before. I grabbed hold of a nearby chair. Staying close to the wall, I made my way to my room.

A couple of hours later, Londaria grew larger out my window. I wondered if a city that big could fall. "I won't let that happen." I had no idea how to keep an aircity in the air, but that didn't mean I couldn't try.

Standing, I walked over to the porthole in my room. The city stretched out before me, but my gaze drifted to the open sky. To the layer of clouds below us. Did dragons lurk nearby, hidden in the clouds? Every part of me, and everything my mother had taught me said to tell someone about the dragons, and especially the riders, but they'd get blamed for the outpost falling.

I didn't know if they had done it, but I didn't think so.

They didn't feel evil. When the outpost slipped, their surprise was as real as my own, and in the end, I had to help them. As my mother always said – guilty people are never surprised.

They *had* taken something. The heavy thing in the bag. But my father said fake ore caused the fall, not a faulty piece of equipment.

The world held so much mystery. So many questions. I wanted answers. But no one told kids anything other than what to do. If I wanted answers, I would have to find them myself.

As we approached the airdocks, I walked to the large circular port-side window in the living room. My mother stood on the docks. The hem of her dress whipped about by the wind, as her gloved-hands interlocked. She looked worried. Hopefully, she'd be angrier at my father than me. *Maybe I would keep the dragonriders to myself.*

When I arrived at the gangplank, my father faced the outer hatch. His foot tapped against the metal plating, and his mouth moved like he was practicing a speech. When Rohl opened the door, he rushed down. My mother crossed to meet him, but he pushed past her, and went straight to the port authority. I started down the gangplank. Each step harder than the one before. My mother waited at the end, but when I got there, she clutched me close.

"I guess you heard about the outpost."

"The Duke informed me." She pulled back and scanned over every inch of me. "Are you hurt?"

"No." I tried not to tell her anything, but one pop of her eyebrow and I crumbled. "Really. I'm fine. I remembered what you said, grabbed hold of the railing, and I was even able to help some…" I knew saying the word dragonrider would not be smart, but I'd already started down this path, I hadn't meant to but it slipped out. Still, I needed to say something. "People. Dogger fired the grappler and I snagged the rope. They pulled me up. It was wobblesmock'n scary though."

She hugged me again. "I'm glad your father was with you."

I nodded.

My father returned. She stood and asked, "What happened."

"Something isn't right." He leaned in, "They were using fake airdrainium."

"What?" She bit her lip, like she always did when deep in thought.

"I found another problem as well."

A black-lacquer carriage gleamed in the sunlight as it stopped before us. Thick gray-white clouds swirled underneath, keeping it off the ground. The door popped opened and gold steps folded down. Lord High Chancellor Rycroft stepped down, his blooming robes squeezing through the narrow opening. He stepped down in front of my father. "Inspector. We are all so thankful everyone is safe, but such dramatics. No need to raise alarms on the crowded docks."

My father removed the rounded-derby from his head. "Lord High Chancellor, I must see the airdrainium chamber. I have found some truly disturbing issues at the outpost." He reached into his pocket and pulled out the small gray stone. "They had fake airdrainium. There's more too. I need to make certain Londaria is safe. We have to alert the other facilities. Begin an investigation."

"Inspector. Please, calm yourself." Lord High Chancellor Rycroft put his arm around my father. "There is no need to start a panic. We will speak with the ore manager, and we will get to the bottom of this, but I have not heard of widespread fake airdrainium. Skye Outpost could be nothing more than a fluke. We will begin an investigation. No need to deviate from our schedules. Your inspection is set for next week."

"I know but…"

"Come, for now we must get your family back to the Duke's residence. I'm certain your son is traumatized from this experience. I will tell the chefs to put cake on the menu for dinner."

My father nodded. "Thank you." He and the Lord High Chancellor stepped off, leaving me staring at their backs. I was fine, I wasn't scared… but cake sounded yummy.

# Chapter 13

The cake was yummy. I didn't want to enjoy it, but they gave me a huge piece because I was traumatized. Even though I was fine, really okay, but the creamy icing… maybe I looked a little upset so I could get a second piece.

As my parents went off to talk, I ran into my room. First to go, I yanked the choking tie from my neck. Next, I was about to crumple up my jacket in the corner, but an archangel soared past my window.

I ran over and pressed against the glass. If the archangels were back maybe the Nightraven was still in Londaria. A figure dressed in all black darted into a shadow across the street.

I knew I shouldn't go. The only thing keeping me from a world of trouble was the tramatic experience I'd just been through. I couldn't ignore the Nightraven. I really wanted to know who he was. Besides, the Nightraven kept showing up at the Duke's home, what if he was really after my father, or the Duke himself? Worse, what if the Nightraven caused the outpost to fall?

"I'll just look, yeah, follow and look."

The constables and archangels rushing around couldn't

find the hidden figure, but I could see them. Didn't that mean it was up to me? The Nightraven darted over to a man-hole and set a device on the cover. A brass arm extended and lifted the iron disk. The figure in black slipped into the street and disappeared.

Now or never. The manhole was right out the side door of the Duke's estate. Forget the tie, but I grabbed my jacket and goggles, and ran out the back of the house. Once in the alley, the dark hole in the ground sent shivers through my body. "Maybe this isn't a good idea." Something deep within me screamed out to know why the Nightraven headed into the lower levels of Londaria. Maybe he was laying a trap for my father? So many mabyes…

I had to find out.

As I debated, the device slid under the manhole cover and started to lowered it into place. I climbed down iron rungs anchored into the wall. The brass arm retracted and the device now clung to underside of the manhole cover. I dropped into a grand hall below the street. Not that I had spent much time in sewers. This metal-plated cavern had segmented pipes lining the walls, and every twenty paces a single gas-lit lantern cast a golden glow.

The familiar sound of footsteps on metal grating pulled my gaze down the tunnel where a shadow slipped around the corner. My heart pounded against my chest and my temples throbbed. I wanted to runaway but something drew me further into the depths. Maybe a giant magnet, because I couldn't stop following the figure in black.

We came to a bridge that led to a door on the far side. The Nightraven slowly stepped across, and I hid behind a crate.

The thin man turned around. A black mask came to a point like a beak. He slipped over to the door. The Nightraven tried to spin the large metal wheel, but it wouldn't budge. Two more yanks on the handle did nothing. I pushed further into the shadows behind the crate, as the Nightraven jumped over the railing.

My mouth dropped. I couldn't believe he'd just tumbled off. I ran to the railing and looked over. The Nightraven landed silently on a bridge several levels below. The door down there wasn't locked and he slipped right through.

"I have to get down. But how?" I looked around for a ladder, but saw nothing, not even any rope.

I couldn't jump. I'd die. Pipes attached to the wall beside me, rose from deep below into the ceiling above. I could climb them, they looked like my steamtree on the Caledonia?" I exhaled. "Easy."

I kept repeating, "Easy," to myself, but one glance over the side, and I knew this was a bad idea. My fingers brushed the pipe which was cool enough to hold. I secured my foot on one segmented joint and grabbed hold of a wall bracket. My foot slid along the pipe to the joint below and my hand followed.

"Don't look down. Do not look…" Something deep within pulled my chin to my chest and I saw the chasm below. My hands became sweaty, and my legs wobbled. My foot slipped from the narrow ledge, and I slid along the pipes trying desperately to grasp any bump.

My foot hit a bend in the pipe, and I gripped two wall brackets to keep from falling any further. Gravity pulled me away from the wall, but I dug my fingers into the pipe and hugged them tight.

Twitching, I paused, and took a moment to breathe. Instead of having the normal thought of, let's go home, my brain needed to know more… Why was the Nightraven slipping into the lower levels the night before inspection?

Behind me, was the bridge to the open door. Slowly, I took my hand off the pipe and reached for a cable anchoring the bridge. I wrapped my leg around and shimmied to the railing. With a quick hop, I popped over railing and rushed to the door.

Inside, I found a series of hallways. A maze, like the back-street labyrinths of Paris d'Laire. The Nightraven was down here, somewhere. I ran down a corridor searching for any sign of the figure in black. A series of interconnected paths led everywhere. Finding this thief would be impossible. Voices echoed down the hall and I froze.

"Where is this bloody valve?" A gravelly voice asked.

"Junction C-19. Should be right around the corner," said a second man.

Sprinting down a hallway away from the voices, I stopped at a plaque on the wall with raised letters. D-3. I exhaled and the lump of fear in my throat dropped back to my stomach.

A wave of pain racked my body, but I wasn't injured. The air felt heavy and I struggled for each breath. Pain struck again, and I realized it wasn't mine. Nearby someone hurt so much I couldn't ignore it.

A faint glow lit up the end of the hallway, around the corner the glow grew brighter than the gas-lamp wall sconces. The door lay slightly open. The Nightraven might have passed this way. A sign above the entrance read – Airdrainium Reactor. As silently as the floor would allow, I moved closer to the light, toward the pain.

I slipped into a large circular room ringed with platforms. A huge machine with large tubes coiled around it emerged from the ceiling holding an inverted pyramid. The crystal wrapped in metal pulsed from within.

Below the pyramid, chained to the floor lay a giant dragon.

# Chapter 14

Golden scales, now tarnished, lay sunken against the bones, as if the dragon hadn't eaten in weeks. Now I understood the pain, and seeing this creature wrenched my heart. A tear streamed down my cheek, and I wiped it away.

Did my father know about this? I shook my head. No way. He might be a stickler for the rules, but I couldn't believe he let a dragon be treated this way. Maybe that's why the Lord High Chancellor kept stalling. This must be a really big secret.

I couldn't take my eyes off the dragon, and hurried down the stairs to the center of the room. Huge chains, secured with locks taller than me, had been strung through thick iron brackets all around the dragon. The large, iron rings I'd seen on the floor of the chamber in Skye Outpost – the ones with the deep scratches in them.

A dragon had been chained at Skye Outpost too. I reached out wondering if this creature was dead, but its chest rose slightly and I stumbled back.

My heart was so wrenched in a vice I couldn't breathe. Tears blurred my vision, and I wanted to scream. How could anyone treat a dragon like this? Any animal. I ran to a lock to see if I could open it. A series of keys and combinations held the thick steel hook in place. The intricate lock looked too complicated to pick, and was so big I'd never cut through.

The chain whined and clanked as the dragon's arm shifted. I froze. I hadn't thought about the fact that I was standing next to a starved creature with teeth large enough to eat me. I spun around, and a large golden eye stared back at me.

"Sorry. I'm not here to hurt you." I put my hands out with my palms up to show I meant no harm. "I want to free you, but I don't have the keys."

The dragon's eye closed as it settled. He knew I couldn't do anything. The life in those eyes burned on my soul. I would never forget.

I reached out, gently touching the dragon's scales. Its immense eye opened again, and watched me through a narrow slit. "Hi." I waved.

Wrinkled skin slipped over the golden orb as the eye slowly closed.

My fingers tingled as energy pulsed within the creature. The lights of the machine above throbbed. A loud buzzing noise mixed with grinding gears and the hiss of hydraulics. The dragon's light dimmed as the machine grew brighter. Tubes drew the dragon's energy out, collecting it in the inverted pyramid.

The Nightraven dropped onto one of the immense locks. Covered in black and wearing a raven's mask, intense eyes stared at me. Seeing the dragon made me forget about the Nightraven, but now he crouched above me.

"Hi." I said.

A forceful voice asked, "What are you doing here?"

"Uhm…Following you." I didn't think I should admit that, but my mother had always taught me to tell the truth.

"Excuse you."

"I was curious and I thought you were going after my mother's dresses. You cannot have them!"

"I don't want dresses!"

I paused, "You don't?"

"No." He motioned to dragon. "You're standing next to the biggest secret of the aircities and you don't even realize it."

I looked at the dragon. This was wrong on so many different levels. But the room had been labeled Airdrainium Reactor. "Where's the Airdrainium?"

"Good, your brain hasn't gone to complete mush."

"Hey."

The Nightraven jumped down and approached. I pulled back into the shoulder of the dragon.

A guard walking the catwalk above stopped and pointed. "The Nightraven!" He pulled a whistle on a chain from a pocket in his vest and held a whistle to his lips.

The Nightraven spun around and pierced the whistle with a dart marked by a tail of black feathers. The guard blew, but no sound emerged. The Nightraven threw two more darts. The guard twisted and dodge them, but not from skill. While the guard tried to un-pretzel himself, the Nightraven leapt to the lock, and then sprang toward the catwalk. Grabbing hold of an iron I-beam, he pulled himself up and hurdled the railing. Once beside the guard, the figure in black twirled, and slammed him to the planking. Sticking the guard with a dart, he went limp, and passed out.

I wanted to run, but my heart froze and my knees wobbled. The Nightraven leapt off the catwalk and landed silently nearby. The guard still lay unmoving on the catwalk. I didn't know, if he was okay, but I knew I was next.

I tripped over the dragon's chain and landed beside a giant chipped claw. The Nightraven rushed up. Reaching into a pouch within the silken belt around his waist, he pulled out a small metal mesh mask with a cloth inside. He poured liquid from a small glass vial over the cloth. I pushed away, but the thief approached. I was about to scream, when another guard walked around the dragon.

"Over here! The Nightraven!" The guard pointed a spear at us.

A faint mumble came from underneath the black mask, but his words were so soft I couldn't tell what was said.

As the guard charged, the Nightraven flipped over the spear, and tumbled past him. Once behind the guard, the masked figure pressed the metal mesh and cloth against the guard's mouth until his eyes rolled back, and he slumped to the floor. I saw my chance to get away, but I couldn't scurry away fast enough.

The heavy chamber door ripped off its hinges and tumbled into the room. I jumped. The dragon shifted and moaned. An archangel soared in and circled the chamber. Gears rotated, extending tawny feathers along the brass-articulated arms. Leather straps wrapped around his chest to a large glowing sphere over his heart. The white cloak whipped about below him.

My heart pounded in my chest, and I feared my soul was about to be ripped from my body. The archangel's eyes burned and jumped from the Nightraven to me. This couldn't be good. *Definitely, all three names kind of trouble, probably even a Mr.*

"I order you to surrender Nightraven. Failure to comply invites death."

I tried to move but the all-white eyes of the archangel held me in place.

He stopped and hovered above me. "Lad, stay put unless you want trouble."

The Nightraven bolted for the far wall and the archangel soared after him. The thief leapt onto the wall and sprang over the winged-man. The archangel slammed into the wall with his knees and hands, leaving four dents in the metal. The Nightraven tumbled and popped up running straight for me.

I held my arms out in protest. The Nightraven lowered his shoulder and scooped me up. I squirmed in protest, but as I raised my head, the archangel chased after us. Kicking my legs and waving my arms sent us tumbling into the hallway. The archangel soared over us, and circled back. The Nightraven grabbed a metal drain cover in the floor, yanked it off, and shoved me inside. I fell through a pipe to the level below. The Nightraven followed and landed on me.

I shimmed out from under him and started to crawl away.

"Don't run," The Nightraven said. "We have to get out of here."

"There's no we. I need to get away."

"Anderax you can't go back. That archangel will figure out who you are, he probably already knows."

"How do you know my name?" I didn't know what to

do. Something familiar in the voice made me pause, but this thief was wanted in every aircity. Grinding metal whined nearby as a hatch opened. Every muscle of mine tensed. Guards, or worse, the archangel would be here in moments.

"We have to go right now." The Nightraven stood up and reached out his hand.

"No way." I ran but chose the wrong direction and found it dead-ended a few steps into my escape. I spun around and pressed my back against the cold metal wall. The Nightraven reached up and unlatched the buckled on the back of the raven mask. My heart beat faster, as long brown hair fell about a female's face. "Mom!"

# Chapter 15

y mother held out her black-gloved hand. "We have to run right now."

I still didn't know what to do, maybe this was a trick of the Nightraven to look like my mother. However, she had the same fire in her eyes, but I paused.

"Anderax, I know this is confusing, but if we don't leave they will capture us both, and they will not let you go. You've seen too much."

"The dragon. We have to help him."

"We can't right now, but we will. Anderax, I'm sorry you had to find out like this, but I need you to be strong and come with me."

I wanted to be strong, for her, for myself, to be a man of adventure, not an inspector! I took her hand, and we started to run. My mother, the Nightraven, led us through a series of hallways. Echoing boot steps thundered down the hall behind us and each strike against the ground rippled terror right through me.

My mother remained calm. She darted through theses tunnels, as if she knew them. We stopped at a hatch with a huge wheel locking it in place. She looked around and opened the door. An archangel stood on the other side. He knocked me back with one wing, and I slammed into the wall. Throwing a punch at my mother, he shoved his fingers into her chest. I'd seen an archangel do the same on the airdocks… where he'd ripped out the man's soul. I screamed. A white light flashed on my mother's belt, and the archangel cried out in agony. He staggered backward gripping his smoldering fingertips.

My mother smiled. She grabbed me and we ran through the hatch. The archangel tried to follow but we slipped under a batch of pipes, and he was too big to pursue.

I looked at her sash belt, at the small bronze and silver device with a circular glass center. I wanted to ask a bunch of questions but the intensity in her eyes looked worse than when she was in her studio. I knew better than to disturb her.

We ran down a set of stairs, and I wondered how many more levels until we reached the clouds. Huge pipes ran above us, and the wind whipped through these halls deafening every other noise.

We stopped at a hatch with DO NOT EXIT written in red paint. My mother pressed her hand against the metal and laid her forehead against the back of her palm. Her eyes darted back and forth, and mumbled to herself. I couldn't hear, but I think she was arguing with herself. She exhaled, then turned to me, and dropped to her knee. Her hands grabbed my shoulders, and as tears filled her eyes. "Anderax, I'm so sorry about this."

"Sorry about what?"

"We have to leave right now." She lowered her head, "I don't know when we'll be back."

"But father?"

"We can't go back for him. We know too much. I'm afraid of what they might do."

I didn't know what to say. Her eyes trembled. They'd always held happiness, but now I saw a deep pain, and tears welling.

"Anderax there is so much you need to know, but I can't tell you here." She smiled. "I'm about to do something really… insane, but it will be okay."

Behind us, the sound of wrenching metal and the clang of the hatch being thrown down the hall, silenced our conversation. It had to be the archangel, only they had the strength to rip off doors.

My mother quickly unrolled the silk wrapped around her waist. She opened the hatch and more wind whipped in. We stepped outside and all I saw were white fluffy clouds churning all around me, darkened by the night. We'd climbed all the way to the bottom of the aircity. My mother wrapped the silk around both of us and secured it with a knot. She pulled my goggles down over my eyes, kissed my head, and leaned over the edge. "Hold on to me."

We tumbled into the darkness and I seized her tight. Over her shoulder I saw the archangel leap off and dive after us. I wanted to close my eyes, but I had to see everything.

I screamed, "archangel," at the top of my lungs, hoping she would hear over the deafening wind.

She nodded, and we continued to fall.

As we punched through the clouds into a clear sky, I watched the archangel still diving behind us. The winged man reached out to snatch us, but a dragon whipped by, and its jaws snapped the archangel's wings off.

I started to wonder if my mother had a plan. I wanted to believe that the dragon would catch us, but the city was getting father away and the dragon still chased the archangel. My heart beat faster and faster until she reached back and released her backpack. A huge silken cloth unfolded, and billowed out above us. We yanked upward, and began to drift on the wind. I tugged on the sash, thankful to be tied to her.

She tugged the cords leading from her backpack to the silk parachute. In the moonlight, the forest had gone from dark green blobs, to individual blobs. Now they grew bigger, and I could see shapes swaying in the night breeze. Below, and getting closer… the ground.

My fear remained in the city. Falling through the air stripped my cares away. My heart beat faster, not from fear, but what I hoped would be my first tree. My mother locked eyes with me and though I barely hear her, she mouthed, "You okay?" I nodded, and she kissed the top of my head.

A flight of seven dragons in a V-formation swooped around us. Each had a rider, except for the biggest dragon, who flew the outside spot on the end of one wing. The rider on the lead dragon wore a long coat with pieces of armor buckled on. His helmet had a visor which covered his face. Nothing like the two I'd met on Sky Outpost, and the guy on the second dragon was twice the size of any other rider. Lead dragonrider stared at us through the shiny metal visor, then banked and raced to the ground.

My mother and I drifted forever, then she pulled on the cords leading to the silken parachute and said, "Prepare for impact."

We raced toward a large clearing, but off in the distance the dark treeline stretched out in both directions. The ground, I was about to touch the ground!

"Lift your legs." My mother said.

I pulled them up, and she bent her knees. We slammed into the ground, and rolled across the grass. My mother popped up and dug in her heels as the silk billowed in the breeze and slid across the grass. She untied the silk sash around us and I dropped into the tall grass. Aromas assaulted my senses from the grass, to the dirt, to the sweet smell coming from the little flowers scattered around me. But in the distance, trees rose up and lifted their branches toward the sky. The leaves swayed in the breeze as all the trees danced with one another.

"Are you okay? Are you injured?" My mother came to my side.

"It's the ground." I grabbed my mouth, and held my breath. When I couldn't hold it any longer I exhaled, and said, "Hold your breath, the plagues!"

"No plagues…" She pulled me against her. "I'm sorry Anderax, I should have brought you down here sooner."

"It's okay, I'm here now." I said muffled through her shirt.

She stood, and I dropped to the ground. A slimy substance lay underneath me. "What is this?"

"Mud. It can't hurt you."

The ground squished between my fingers and soaked my knees. I molded it with my hands and poked my finger deep into its squishy center. The mud had such a sweet, musky aroma. I'd never smelled anything similar.

My mother stared up into the night's sky. "Come on, we have to get moving before more archangels descend." She lifted me up and put me on my feet. "Start gathering the parachute, I'll roll up the cords."

The huge cloth fought me every inch, enwrapping my arms in silk as I rolled it up. The wind kept pulling it away, but as I'd seen the crew of the Caledonia do, I wrapped it up quickly by keeping it close to my body. I handed my mother the bundle, and she stuffed it into the bag on her back.

She looked up toward Londaria, a dark spot high in the sky, with a few lights twinkling like stars. "We have to keep moving. The dragons chased the archangels away but they'll return."

"How do you know so much?"

"I'm the Nightraven," she said with a wink. "I've been outsmarting archangels for years."

The dragons swooped out of the sky, flared their wings, and landed around us. Their claws dug into the mud as if gripping the ground was the only thing keeping them from launching back into the sky.

The lead rider dismounted. His long dark blue jacket whipped about in the wind, except where armored plates kept it pressed against his body. Brown boots rose to his knee with armored bracers on the outer calf. He pulled off his silver helmet, and ran his hand over his head pulling the long dark hair from his sweaty brow. "Beatrix," he extended his hand. "What happened, we weren't expecting to hear from you for another month."

My eyes popped open. My mother knew a dragonrider. Plus, he knew her whole name. I'd only heard her middle name once before. My father used it once a couple of years ago. But now she was the Nightraven, and I didn't know what to think.

My mother reached out her hand. "Change of plans. We have a complication."

"I see that." The rider peered around my mother. He stepped toward me and extended his hand. "You must be Anderax, I'm Captain Duncain."

"Hi." I shook his hand. My father said none of this was real, but a dragon and the rider stood in front of me. *Wait until I tell him all about this.* The air rushed out of my lungs – I didn't know when that would be. My mother never talked about her childhood, but she obviously knew these people. As my heart sank a question jumped out, "What about my father?"

The silence lasted long enough to become uncomfortable. Finally, my mother knelt down, "I don't know yet, but *we* can't go back to Londaria."

"Because you're the Nightraven, and the dragon they have chained up."

She smiled, "That's right," but her expression faded. "I'm sorry you had to see that."

"Why are they doing that to the dragon?"

"What are they doing to the dragon?" Duncain asked.

My mother answered both of us, "I don't know exactly."

A large silver dragon swooped in and landed. The dragon folded back its wings and a man with white hair and beard dismounted. He rushed out and embraced my mother. She looked stunned as he wrapped her in his arms, but she wiggled free, and hugged him back.

"It's good to see you, lass. I imagine this isn't a social visit."

"We found something horrible. The archangels discovered

us, and I had no choice. We had to jump."

He pulled back from her and turned to me. He might have the hair of an old man, but not the face. I'd seen countless vacant eyes on droopy faces, but this guy had strong eyes and a deep wrinkled brow. A barrel chest pushed open his long red coat. His jacket also had pieces of armor strapped on, but his were richly decorated with dragons, and trimmed with gold. If it weren't for the cloud-white hair, I'd never believe he was elderly.

"And who might you be young man?" His eyes fixed on me.

His thick accent was almost hard to understand, and his deep voice sent shivers all through me. I reached my hand out and said, "I'm Anderax Grayvenhorn."

"Odin, an old friend of your mother."

My mother's expression hardened. "We'll catch up later. This is serious. Londaria is using dragon mana instead of airdrainium."

"What!" He snapped his head toward her. His eyes widened. "Barbarians."

"I'm pretty certain the archangel figured out who I was and I know he could identify Anderax. I didn't know what else to do but flee."

"You did the right thing. What's coming is not the kind of thing the boy should endure." Odin pulled his fingers through his beard. "We need to get out of here. Let's go to the academy, and figure this out."

"I have to get back." My mother looked up at Londaria. "I have to warn my husband, and the Caledonia."

Odin roared in a thick drawl, "I won't allow it!"

My mother fired back, "You don't have a choice. I'm going!" She paused. "I have to."

"Then we'll all go. We'll lay siege to Londaria."

The riders and the dragons cheered around us.

My mother didn't laugh, in fact, her face hardened. "We don't even know where they might be keeping him."

"All the more reason for a flight of dragonriders to join you."

"The risk is too great. I'll be better on my own." She gripped Odin's sleeve. "I need you to look after my son."

"We'll keep Anderax safe, you don't even have to ask. I'll train him with the other cadets."

I'd listen to them stunned and unsure what they were talking about, but he said cadet. Were the smaller, younger riders I'd seen on Skye Outpost cadets? Could I be a dragonrider? I smiled. Training with the other cadets sounded like fun. My mind began to imagine a dozen different scenarios, training, flying lessons, and more. My body stiffened, would I get a cool coat?

"You will not. I didn't bring him down here to become a dragonrider."

"But he is of age. Soon, he will have to learn the truth and make his own decisions."

"He is just a boy."

"A few seasons from being a young man."

"Anderax is air dweller, not a grounder."

"Neither were you."

"I don't have time to argue, Odin. I'll be back when I can. No more than a month."

My heart dropped. The pain of the empty space left behind made my fingers numb. She was leaving me. As my heart began to race, it beat against my chest so hard I thought I might have bruises.

She knelt down and clutched me close. "I have to go back and check on your father, on the Caledonia. You're going to go with these dragonriders. Odin will take good care of you. I will be back soon."

Tears streamed down my cheeks, but I didn't say a word. She hugged me tight once again, and I clung on hoping to never let go.

"Safe journeys!" Odin wrapped his arms around my mother and me like a bear and lifted us off the ground. "Duncain and ShadowClaw will get you back onto Londaria."

She chuckled but protested until he set us down. "Just keep him safe. I know my son, and archangels are relentless."

She kissed my head and ran over to ShadowClaw. Duncain climbed into his saddle and helped my mother to get on behind him. She raised her hand to say goodbye to me. I waved, but I didn't know when I'd see her again.

She put her hand on Duncain's shoulder, and called Odin over. Though they were several feet away, I could still hear them. Odin patted her leg. "You know everyone here would die before letting that boy get taken off by an archangel."

"Don't tell him." My mother said.

Oden cocked his head. "Where you've gone, or who he is?"

She paused and then looked at me. "I will be the one to explain who he is, but not tonight."

*Who am I?*

Odin nodded and walked back to me, he extended his

hand and it covered my entire shoulder. "Come one, lad. Time to introduce you to the Highland Dragon Academy."

"A *dragon* academy!" I gasped. "What's that?"

Odin patted my back. "Where riders train with dragons."

A woman standing beside a red dragon, said sharply, "They're hidden all over the world. Hidden from the world above and those who dwell on the ground. We train riders and raise dragons."

Not only were dragons real, but there were schools to learn to become a dragonrider.

Odin locked eyes with me. "This is a secret place. I'll need you to keep that secret or one of the dragons will have to eat you."

Every muscle seized up as the thought of those giant jaws closing over me. "I won't tell," I blurted out.

"Good."

"Odin." One of the dragon's said.

"Oh, I was just having a little fun with the lad."

Dragons talked? Maybe I heard the wind, but I was pretty certain the big blue dragon had moved his mouth.

Odin leaned closer. "I see a question in those eyes."

How did he know, and what did a question look like? I had a thousand of them. Starting with do dragons talk, but only one came out. "Is that plague fog?" I pointed at thick cloud rolling into the clearing.

Odin threw back his head and laughed. "No."

"But aren't you worried about the plagues?"

"There hasn't been a case of plague in a hundred years. You hear too much aircity propaganda."

*A hundred years?* "But the nobles freaked out last spring.

Everyone in Londaira wore masks for a month." I knew the nobles were out of touch, but how much were they wrong about?

# Chapter 16

The largest dragonrider, still on his mount, pointed toward the sky, "Archangels."

"Lady Z, Olgarth distract them. I will lead the others off. Travel the forests and meet back at the academy." Odin pointed at me. "The lad will need a rider."

The biggest dragon, the one without a rider stepped up. Even in the dark his blue leathery scales captured the moonlight making him look so majestic. The large dragon loomed over my head and there was something familiar about his eyes. The dragon's head lowered down until the horns on his chin poked the ground. "He will be safe with me."

The dragons and their riders fired shocked glances between them. Odin cocked his head to the side, "He might not be able to ride without a rider."

"I see dreadnaughts too. You may have to fight. I will focus on getting the lad to safety."

My mouth dropped. I'd wondered what dragons might be like. They didn't just talk they were smart, caring, and more eloquent than I am. So many questions flooded my mind. Too many to write down for later. However, no matter how hard I tried, I couldn't ask them. My eyes would not look away from this dragon. Watching his mouth move around sharp teeth. The way his whole face shifted and expressed. *Wow.*

Odin nodded. He put his hand on my shoulder and said, "Anderax, this is IronCloud. He'll take good care of you."

"I get to ride on a dragon?"

"Yes, and very soon too." He grabbed me, hoisting me up the side of the blue dragon. "Hook your foot into the stirrup, and lock into the saddle."

Getting my feet in was the easy part. The saddle hugged the rider, and if I was an adult, it would hold me quite snugly, but I was a skinny kid. After strapping the belt around my waist, and tightening it as mush it could, I could slip out without unbuckling it, if I wanted.

Odin tugged on the belt, he twisted it around a nob on the saddle which did secure it a little more. "Hold real tight to the pommel and you'll be fine."

As bright-white beams from the airship's searchlights cast down on the field, each dragon leapt into the sky. IronCloud and I stayed low and flew off away from the others. Odin and the other dragons circled up toward the airships.

The wind bit against my cheeks and nose. Pulling my goggles up over my eyes allowed me to see. I blew hot air into my hands to keep warm as I often did when standing on the sundeck of my steamtree. However, none of it matter. I didn't feel any pain when we dropped out of the clouds and the world lay below me once again.

In the dead of night, a river of stars dazzled across the clearing sky. Below, the ground undulated through varying shades of black. Yet the occasional orange glow came from within small houses scattered across the land. It was a different view from the airships, no chugging engines or whistling steam pipes to distract me, and being closer to the ground brought more detail to every sight. From a dragon's back the whole world lay before me and anything was possible.

I thought the Caledonia had personality, a quirky sense of humor, she'd be fickle one day but always came through when trouble was near, but dragons had so much more. The dragon breathed, his sides expanded and contracted with each beat of his heart beneath me. As his wings flapped the rest of his body reacted, and I shifted back and forth in my saddle to this rhythm.

I wouldn't trade this for anything. "I wish my mom could be here." I said out loud without thinking.

IronCloud glanced back at me. "Do you see the moon?"

I paused and said, "Of course."

"So does she."

I looked up at the large sphere hanging high in the sky. My mother and I used to track its phases on a calendar in her workshop. Those nights felt like a lifetime ago, but staring up at the moon made me think of her.

"Your mother is looking up at that moon and thinking of you."

"Really?"

"Of course," IronCloud's lips curled up in a smile. "She's the Nightraven. The moon is her friend."

I stared up at the moon and knowing she was somewhere looking at the same spot in sky eased the ache in my heart. "I used to ask my dad if the moon needed airdrainium to rise into the sky."

IronCloud chuckled and said, "How remarkable, a mind

filled with wonder and possibility." He paused. "What was his answer?"

"He told me to stop making nonsense."

IronCloud snorted. "Imagination is never nonsense. It's the fabric of the universe."

"What? There's nothing between the stars. That's why it's black."

"What!" His deep growl shook the saddle. "The universe is infinite." We soared up toward the stars. "Meaning anything is possible. The space between stars is filled with imagination. If magic is thought, emotion, and focus combined into a single moment, then imagination and magic are the same."

"I'd never thought of it like that before."

"That's because you're not a dragon."

# Chapter 17

IronCloud banked toward the full moon. He flapped his wings three times, and we soared toward the horizon. I never wanted to come down. I stretched my arms and yawned. My eyes watered and I had trouble keeping them open…

I snapped awake and gripped the pommel. I'd dozed off, but for how long? I leaned over to see if IronCloud had noticed but he was focused on the ground.

Sunlight spilled over edge of the world, illuminating the waving grass, casting shadows over the fields, and breaking up in the trees. Dawn. I'd slept for hours. I couldn't believe I hadn't fallen off. "I must have been tired."

"It's a skilled rider who can sleep in the saddle."

"I assume you kept me from falling. Thanks."

He glanced back. "I just didn't make any hard banks."

Wow, I did have skills. I was good at climbing, and getting into trouble, but I never really had a real skill before. I was just a kid, but I was riding the biggest of dragons, and could sleep in the saddle. *What else was I good at?*

After several minutes, IronCloud descended. The leafy giants danced with the morning light as they swayed in the breeze. I couldn't stop staring. I reached out, and leaned so far over that I slipped. I snatched the worn leather-wrapped pommel and strained my muscles to pull myself back up. My heart slammed against my chest and I was fully awake now. "Maybe I will just wait until we get closer."

"That might be best." IronCloud chuckled.

We crossed over a small triangular clearing in the forest and IronCloud banked hard and spiraled down. His wings flared, he stretched his feet out, and I made certain everything cleared the trees. IronCloud lurched as he landed, but I easily remained in the saddle.

Towering pillars of bark rose out of a thick blanket of leaves. Their branches stretched out, forming a web of wood around me. Beyond this ring of trees surrounding the clearing, more stood, like an army marching across the land. "Oak trees!"

"Yes. Humans. You give the tree a name, but you still don't see it as alive."

"They're alive! Astounding!" I hopped off the saddle and couldn't stop spinning around. Each tree was different. Some had a single thick trunk, others split near the base and stretched out in any number of directions. These giants rose a hundred feet into the sky while others, younger ones I guess, reached in-between for any glimpse of morning light. Together, they formed a thick canopy which kept the forest in darkness even as sunlight flooded the land.

"You really like trees." IronCloud settled down, tucking his wings and tail.

"These are the first I've ever seen up close." I walked over and placed my hand on the gnarled bark.

"What?" IronCloud spit a ball of fire and pushed his front

legs up off the ground. "Your first tree?"

"I've spent my whole life in the air." I ran my hand along the rough bark and unlike metal and stone it wasn't cold to the touch. In fact, it felt warm as if it pulsed inside.

"These are some good ones. Trust a dragon, you can't spend your whole life in the sky, sometimes you have to land and explore a cave."

"I've never been in cave either, but I've been in the undercity. I think it's kind of the same thing."

"I've never been in the undercity, but I doubt it." IronCloud chuckled and shook his head. He settled back down on his front paws.

I wondered what he meant and almost asked what caves were like, but I realized we were alone. How were we the first to arrive when we took the long way? I walked around and checked each side but didn't see anyone. I stopped in front of IronCloud. "Where is everybody?"

The dragon lifted his long neck and scanned the forest.

"This is the academy, right?" I didn't see an academy, just trees.

IronCloud stroked his chin. "Wait, maybe not."

"What do you mean?"

"Odin said to use the forest to hide. He probably meant to take the forest to the Highland Academy. Maybe he meant Sherwood Academy. It's hidden in a forest. I, however, was thinking about the Arthurian Academy."

I scratched my head. "How many academies are nearby?"

"Three. Well, two. The Highland and Sherwood Academies are friendly rivals, and the Arthurian Academy was put to ruin long ago."

"I think we're supposed to be at the Highland Academy." My hand rested on my hips. "We're in the wrong place."

"We'll be safe if we can get inside, but the entrance is hidden and sealed."

"That doesn't sound easy."

"Nothing fun ever is."

I stared at the dragon. We were nowhere near the others, and worse, we were all alone if the archangels attacked. As I stepped toward the edge of the clearing. Worry whipped up inside me like a tornado, and every noise in the forest made me jump.

I walked back to IronCloud and my racing heart eased. I nodded my head and smiled. "What do I need to do?"

IronCloud lit up and pointed up to the canopy. "At the top of that tree is a door."

# Chapter 18

A bounciness rose up in my legs. "You want me to climb a tree?"

"That's right."

I jumped and threw my arms into the air. "I get to climb a tree!" I don't think my feet came back to the ground, I floated on joy.

"You might want to get started its pretty high up there."

My eyes wouldn't leave the tree but I asked, "What do I do?"

He raised a finger for each point. "Get to the door. Use the key to open the door. Enter the academy and open the dragon door."

"Do you have the key?"

He pointed up. "It's up there."

"They left the key next to the door? That doesn't seem very safe?"

"How many people walk into a forest looking for a door in a tree?"

I nodded. "Good point."

IronCloud pointed at the tallest tree in the grove. I searched every inch with my eyes, but no door. "Are you sure?"

"Of course. I'm a dragon."

I walked over to the base of the tree, the thickest in the clearing. Huge roots wove through the dirt like dragon talons gripping the earth. Gnarled knots and a web of branches formed a ladder to the top. "I think I can do this."

IronCloud's deep voice washed over me. "I know you can."

I reached up and my fingers gripped the rough bark. I put my foot on one of the roots and pulled myself up. I grabbed the next couple of knots to reach the cradle of the lowest branch. I looked over at IronCloud. He encouraged me to continue with a gesture of his head.

With a nod, I put both hands around the next branch and pulled my legs up. Wrapping them around, I hoisted myself onto the branch. I sat for a moment and looked around, the ground was far below. I still had a long journey above me, but I was higher than IronCloud was tall.

*I am in a tree. Better than that, I'm climbing a tree!* The trees before me swayed in the wind. The tree I sat on moved and I held on. The leaves whipped about, some breaking loose to drift on the wind.

Brushing the bits of bark from my hands, I stepped onto the next limb and spiraled up around the tree using the thick branches like stairs. Halfway up I rested for a moment by slinging my legs on either side of the branch. Below me, on the backside, another large tree had fallen and wedged itself against this one. Looking out, the forest grew so thick I couldn't see more than a few feet.

The higher I climbed the more my heart pounded. I didn't have a problem with the heights, I lived on airships, but looking down made my stomach queasy. I reached up and grabbed a broken branch. It snapped off, and I fell.

IronCloud hopped up and charged the tree. I hit the branch I'd been standing on, and it slid up to armpit. I grabbed hold and steadied myself against the trunk.

The dragon's voice rose from below. "Anderax, are you okay?"

I pulled up onto the branch and rolled on top. I waved to the dragon who now stood below me. "I'm fine."

Climbing up to the branch above, I paused to let the muscles in my arm loosen. I reached for the next limb and heard a high-pitched squeal. A small furry animal with a big fluffy tail jumped off, right over my head. Landing on the trunk, it scampered around the trunk and disappeared. *Oh wow, what was that? My mind sped through my tutor's talks until the day we learned about trees. Squirrel. That was a squirrel.* My heart pounded in my chest. My lungs burned, and I couldn't slow my breathing. I ached, and the next branch made me wonder what other deathtraps remained.

Seeing IronCloud below me made me wonder where my courage had gone. Whenever dragons were around, I could do anything, but the higher I climbed the more my courage faded. I took a deep breath and swallowed the fear.

The branches grew thinner the higher I went, but they still held my weight. As I pulled myself up to the next level, I found broken boards nailed to the tree and a thick metal bolt sticking out of the bark.

"I think I found something," I yelled. "There are boards nailed up here."

"Sounds like the right spot."

I scanned the tree and didn't see a door, but I did find a

keyhole. Cut into the bark I saw the familiar circle on top of a triangle – the classic keyhole.

IronCloud mentioned a key and said it would still be up here. I searched around hoping that it hadn't been kept on the platform. A glint of morning sunlight reflected off the trunk above me. A metal loop had been fitted around the top of the tree. The thinnest branch held the key.

Slowly, I climbed higher, testing each branch before committing to the next. Quickly the limbs became too thin to stand on and each one I grabbed shook the whole tree. But the key was still further away than my tallest reach.

I cupped my hand around my mouth and aimed at the dragon. "I'm not tall enough to reach the key. What do I do?"

"You're the rider, figure it out." IronCloud walked back into the clearing and settled onto the grass. "I'm just a dragon; I certainly can't get up in a tree.

*He's right. Getting the key was up to me.*

I thought about cutting off the top of the tree, but that would hurt the tree, and the key might fall to the ground. I considered using a stick. I even searched for the right one. None were thick enough, they'd bend.

Bending.

If I pulled on the tree, I could drop the key off the branch and catch it.

I reached up as high as I could, and pulled on the top branch. It bent over further and further, the key dangled from the metal loop. The ring slid to the end of the branch and I held out my other hand. With a little jiggle the key slipped off and landed right in my palm.

I climbed back down to the keyhole. The tree swayed back and forth in a strong wind. I closed my hand around the key, and pressed myself against the trunk. With a quick turn of my head, I looked out over the canopy. A web of branches stretched out across the forest. The trees danced in the morning light, and I had climbed one! The scene was beautiful. I could stand here forever letting the wind pass around me.

But I had a job to do.

I put the key into the keyhole. It fit, and I smiled.

Two turns to the left and I heard a click. Hidden in the cracks of the bark was the outline of a door. Rectangular in shape, the door opened inward as I pushed on the outside. Dust kicked up creating a choking cloud. Dusty spider webs torn by the opening door hung from the ceiling. I stepped inside the trunk and found a room atop this tree.

The central core had been removed leaving the thick outer rind of the tree. Two small chairs sat next to a small, dust-covered, wood-burning stove that hadn't shed any warmth in a long time.

"IronCloud said I had to find the entrance to the academy." I started searching for another door. The place was tiny, so it didn't take long to search.

Nothing. No door, no keyhole, not even a crack with a breeze.

It has to be here. I didn't climb a tree, and find a hidden door only to be stopped now. I stood against the wall. The rough bark bit into me, and I checked my hand for splinters. The crew often got a sliver of wood in their skin. Luckily, I didn't have one.

Across from me lay a symbol carved into the rough wood of the inner trunk. The rider had been worn smooth by the touch of countless hands. I walked over and ran my fingers along the grooves. The symbol showed a rider and dragon over a castle with a sword coming out of a stone in the center of the building.

It had to mean something I just had to figure out what.

My eye kept going back to the worn rider. Deep grooves surrounded the figure. Maybe it was a button? I pressed hard against the rider and heard the slightest click come from the floor.

Several boards popped up. I pulled on the edge and the floor lifted up revealing a spiral staircase descending through the trunk. "I found it!"

# Chapter 19

A mirror hung on a pivoting bar above the stairs. I angled it to catch the sunlight and a column of light cast down through the center of the tree. The stairs spiraled down the inner wall of the trunk, made of the carved wood from what used to fill this space. The center remained opened.

My fingers bounce along the wall as I ran down the stairs. Within moments I was at the bottom. "The stairs were easier than the branches." I leaned my head back and stared up at the stairs and column of light. I could be standing in any castle. "Wait. Are all trees like this on the inside?" I'd never read that before.

The last step led to a tunnel. The fallen tree I'd seen resting against the back. The thoughts of where this might lead made me jump up and down. All I knew is that somewhere down there was a dragon door, and I had to open it. I couldn't see the end of the tunnel, but IronCloud was counting on me.

The fear that had gripped me faded, and though, the tunnel was dark, light pierced the ceiling. I didn't fear the dark. A muffled rustling and the low echo of a dragon's grumble beyond the wooden wall shook the tree. IronCloud must be sitting on the ground outside.

"Open the door, and I won't be alone." Knowing that IronCloud sat outside melted my worries away.

I smacked the roof of the tunnel with the palm of my hand and a sturdy thump echoed along the walls. The passage creaked and groaned with each step but remained solid. A long bug with a hundred legs crawled through the wood and ran along the wall to a different hole. I pushed against the opposite wall, but continued on. My spine got all wobbly but I tried to shake it off.

Deeper into the unknown, any fear turned to fascination. I slid my hands over every nook and knot, awed by this world of wood. The earthy smell of this place made each breath better than the next. Bugs crawled over and through, creating a whole community in the tree. All the different levels reminded me of the aircities.

At the end of the wooden tunnel, I found a circular door made of thick knotted boards. A tarnished brass handle sat in the center. I reached out and my fingers closed around the cool metal. It didn't budge. I turned the handle and pushed harder. The whine of metal grinding echoed through the wood.

The door swung open, and I tumbled into an underground chamber. The huge arching passage wound around a corner and could easily fit a dragon without his wings touching the walls.

"The dragon door?" I turned around and froze. The door had been made not of planks of wood, but of whole trunks lined up next to each other. Each had been capped and reinforced with thick iron plates. The door stretched from one side of the chamber to the other and rose thirty feet to the ceiling. "How am I going to open that?"

A large spoked-wheel with a thick iron chain sat on one wall and connected to the massive door. A lever moved a thick metal bar that held the wheel in place. Cobwebs and a layer of dust clung to everything. Rust had tarnished all the metal, and I wasn't even certain these old mechanics would still turn.

I grabbed the lever and pulled. It wouldn't budge, and I tried harder until my muscles strained and I had to stop. *Not good.* How was I supposed to open a door that wouldn't budge? *Especially a door the size of an airship.*

"IronCloud is counting on me." I checked over the mechanism to make certain I hadn't missed anything. I brushed the dust off the base of the lever and pulled out clumps of debris.

I shook my head. The lever's slot wasn't behind but in front. I'd been pulling when I should have been pushing. Breathing nothing but old musty air made me cough, but I pushed with everything I had. The metal arm groaned and creaked as it slid forward. The metal bar slid out from the wheel and I pulled on the wooden spokes. It slowly spun pulling the chain. I crossed my fingers, hoping the door would open. No one had used this place in a long time.

The huge door of tree trunks lowered slowly and steadily like a draw bridge. Sunlight rushed in and I raised my arm to shade my eyes. As a huge shadow fell over me, I lowered my hand. IronCloud stood backlight by the sun. Particles of dust shimmered around him like a powerful aura. "Astounding."

"Good work!" IronCloud stepped inside with a distant far-off expression in his large eyes.

"Thanks." I pointed toward the tree tunnel. "Best tree for a first-timer."

"It used to be the watchtower, a lookout post to know when to open the gate." He stopped in front of me and smiled. "Congratulations on climbing your first tree."

I nodded. "The stairs were the best part. Do all trees have stairs?"

The dragon laughed. A bellowing sound filled the chamber and the rumbled through the parts we hadn't seen yet. "No. Only the ones carved by riders."

"Astounding." Chiseled walls supported a ceiling of massive wooden rafters. IronCloud was right. Riders had gone to a lot of work crafting every part of this structure. "What is this place?"

"This was the first dragon academy hidden just a song's distance from the castle." Further in, the walls and ceiling changed to rock, and the carvings became more elaborate. "King *Pendragon* wrote the Pax Draconis. The first treaty with dragons. He became the first to ride a dragon in almost a thousand years. The first Peacecrafter."

My feet refused to take another step. "Ast-"

"Astounding, yes I know." He nudged me. "Close your mouth."

I twisted and snapped my jaw shut. Then sped forward to catch up, unable to wipe the smile from my face. We turned the corner and the wall was lined with large stalls. "The dragon stables," IronCloud said.

At the end of hall, I found the base of a grand staircase

leading up into the rock. A carved dragon pillar sat on each step and supported a stone and bronze railing. The globes at the end of each banister had tops so polished the landmasses had worn away.

IronCloud's voice echoed behind me. "Touched thousands of times by riders for luck."

I reached out my hand, running my fingers over the polished metal. The cold bronze sent a jolt through my arm. I shook my hand to make the tingling stop. "What is that?" I asked, as I stepped to the wall with strange symbols and figures carved into the rock.

"Rune writing along with images of the knights and dragons."

"What do they say?"

IronCloud leaned in and studied the alcove. He pointed to first panel. "This is a blessing for dragons. *Long life, strong tailwinds, and herds of cattle.*" He pointed to the other side. "That one is a blessing for the riders. *Live life with honor, courage, and in duty to mankind.*"

My head spun. Those words, the most profound I had ever heard. I couldn't stop thinking about this place. King Arthur and his knights had walked these halls. The stones had so many stories to tell, my mind couldn't stop imagining each and every one.

"I'll never forget those words." I wanted to write them down, but I just kept repeating them so I'd remember.

IronCloud pointed to the rest of the rune panels. "These are incantations to protect the dragon and riders."

"What?"

"Magic spells."

I scratched my head. "Like real magic?"

"Of course. You know about dragons, right?"

"No, until a few days ago, I didn't even know dragons were real. They don't talk about dragons very nicely in the aircities."

He nodded. "Dragons are the ones who taught humans to use magic." IronCloud settled down on his paws and tucked his tail around him. "Long ago, high up on the rooftop of the world, humans befriended dragons. Eventually, dragons taught them about magic. An age of discovery followed. Humans stopped running all over the place and settled into villages. Each generation's bloodline drifted farther from the first friends. Humans used magic, but forgot to thank the dragons for the knowledge. Out of fear and misunderstanding, they sent dragon hunters. The bond between men and dragons was severed."

Until this place.

"That's right. You catch on quick."

I smiled and tilted my head. "But if King Arthur made peace why are we at war?"

"It has been many generations since that friendship and once again the humans fear dragons. It was so bad many humans took to the sky."

That made so much sense. "The nobles of every aircity I've ever visited hate dragons. They blame you for all the troubles on the ground and fear being attacked whenever they travel."

"The *hi-nobles* developed a fog to kill all the dragons. Two centuries ago they raised their cities into the sky and released the plague. The problem was the fog also affected the humans. They killed many dragons sleeping in their caves, but many of us flew away. The war began."

"I had no idea."

"Most don't. Including many of the dragons flying today."

"That's sad. My dad is always saying that history is important. He says he couldn't do his job unless people recorded their results before him."

"He has a good point."

A cool wind whipped through the stalls stirring up dust and cobwebs. It brushed past me and whipped up my hair. The breeze rushed up the stairs with a howling echo. Up the passage, it sounded like spirits or ghosts running through the halls. Curiosity was killing me, wondering what lay at the top.

"You must continue."

"But I don't want to leave you."

"You must see if you can climb those stairs." He stretched his head out laying it on the ground. "The spirits call you."

"I don't know. I mean, they're ghosts."

The dragon's eyes popped open. "Ghosts can't hurt you."

"But they can scare you."

"Fear is the mind worrying. By mastering fear, you can do anything."

"Will you come with me? I'm not as afraid when you're around."

IronCloud's head rose. "Now that *is* astounding."

"Why?"

"Fear oozes from dragons like an odor. Most people feel a quickening of their heart. Sweat forms on their palms and brow. Most scream as they run away. Riders overcome this emotion through discipline."

"You take my fear away."

"Fascinating. I've only known one other who spoke those words."

"Who?"

"The last king of this land."

"The Cloud King, my tutors taught me about him."

IronCloud snarled, and I stepped back. In his low guttural voice, he said, "If you want a real history lesson head up those steps."

I stood up and walked over to the stairs. My mind raced over everything I might find, the good and the haunted. I pulled myself together and with everything I had, I placed my foot on the first step. The second was easier and by the fourth, I was walking normally.

The stairs rose straight through the rock to a large open room. I thought I'd be standing in darkness but sunlight shone through the shattered stones above. I stood in ruins, overgrown with vines and grass. Several trees rose through the building, their roots hanging over and around the stones. Several crumbled statues stood in this hall. Knights in armor with a dragon design.

I picked up the hilt of a broken stone sword. I wanted to keep the trinket, but it felt wrong to take it from the shattered knight. The walls of the main hall had been carved like the stables below, with pictures of dragons and riders on every panel. Dragon runes ran along the top of the walls.

I climbed over chunks of ceiling stones as I walked through the broken corridors. A statue of a dragonrider stood in an alcove at the end. It was a woman. She stood in a regal pose with her sword at her side and a real lance in her hand. The armor was segmented with a large dragon curled on her breastplate. Her helmet had a raised visor with slots to see through, but it was her face that captivated me. She had a strong expression, with a slight smile which made me wonder who she was. Stones from the fallen ceiling covered the base of the statue. I saw the corner of a bronze plaque peeking out from behind the rock, and rolled it out of the way.

The plaque held a name – Boudicca Kingsgard – "My mother was a Kingsgard. She told me once when I asked about her family."

# Chapter 20

My fingers traced over the name cast in bronze. I wondered who this woman might have been. She had to be important, only important people had statues. Plus, this one stood alone in a place of honor. She wore armor. Was she a warrior like my mother?

But what did it mean? Did I come from a long line of warriors? A happy thought I held on to. I was a dragonrider, from a line of dragonriders. At least I could hope. I thought I'd never be more than an aircity inspector, but now the world was filled with possibility. I could do anything… with a dragon at my side.

The wind stirred my coat. A haunted howl rode the breeze and sent shivers through my body. I wanted to run back to my courage boosting dragon, but that's not what a rider would do. Taking a deep breath, I followed the sound deeper into the ruins.

A light in the shadows drew my eye to a far room. The single shaft headed the wrong direction to be from the sun and hovered off the ground. It certainly didn't act like any sunray I'd ever seen.

Each step thundered off the stones as I set my foot down. The sound rippled through my body screaming for me to run away. My boots felt glued to the stone as I tried to pick them up. My heart raced. My eyes darted from one sound to the next. High-pitched voices buzzed all around me. I spun on my heel. "Who's here?" I asked, hoping I wouldn't get an answer. A tiny globe of light whizzed by. I wasn't certain if it came from behind me or the shadows in front of me. I thought ghosts only came out at night.

Entering the room, the faint glow came from a small sphere sitting on top of a contraption. A thick carpet of spongy grass spread out beneath me. Rock walls surrounded me and formed a dome above.

The sphere brightened as I stepped closer. Around the contraption lay a ring of mounded grass. Wide pillow top mushrooms dotted the darker green patch. In the center, vines had grown around the handcrafted iron tower. Twisted rods formed three legs that wrapped around a wood and metal device. The sphere of light sat on top held by the ends of three iron rods.

"Odd. No dust. No cobwebs." I stepped over the ring and studied this contraption.

Whispers erupted around me as I spun around trying to see where they came from. Buzzing sounds whipped by in the darkness but always behind me. I kept turning trying to see and caught only glimpses of color.

I pressed myself against the iron contraption. Three balls of light froze in midair, then scattered in every direction. Whispers exploded all around me. Behind one of the mushrooms a small head poked up with a long tuft of violet hair. Large eyes framed by pointy ears stared back at me. Thin wing membranes twitched behind her, and tiny fingers gripped the spongey edge.

*A fairy? Wow.* I lit up. My mother read many fairy tales to send me to sleep.

The creature hopped up onto the mushroom. She had thin limbs and crouched in the center of the mushroom cap.

I leaned closer. Too close. Her wings beat rapidly. The faster they moved the brighter her inner violet light glowed from within and spilled out through her wings. She became almost completely light and fluttered around me.

Hundreds of lights filled the room and swirled around me. Stunned by the beauty, I didn't move.

The lights grew bolder and flew right up to my face. They pulled at my coat, at the shoulder strap of my bag, and even tugged on my hair. One tugged at the top of my ear trying to make it pointy. Voices filled the air, but were too high-pitch to understand. Listening carefully, I heard some clearly.

"Send the man away," said one.

"He isn't a man, just a boy," said another.

"Looks like a rider to me," said a third.

"The spirits sent him."

"Smell him – We should help him."

"Let's infect his mind with madness."

I didn't like that last one and tried to see which light said it.

After the thorough examination, a violet light landed beside me on the contraption. "Are you friends with spirits?"

I didn't know what to say. How do you answer a little creature that might make give you madness? "I don't think so, but I'm not against spirits."

The fairy eyed me and rubbed her pointy chin. "Why are you here?"

"A dragon brought me."

A collective, "Oooooooo," rose up from all the lights around me.

She spread her arms and pointed to the ground. "Well, why didn't you say so, but this isn't a dragon academy anymore. It's a fairy academy."

"Oh, I didn't know, I was just taking a look around because—"

"The spirits sent you, we know."

"Do you know why?" I asked. They were the only people around, and it might be my only chance.

"Not sure yet," she said, putting her hands on her hips

I wasn't certain if any of this made sense. Maybe they were messing with me, playing with my mind before infecting me with the madness?

The little fairy pointed at me. "What is your name?"

"Anderax."

She flew up and grabbed my eyelid with her tiny fingers. Pulling it up, she stared into my eye as if searching for something. I froze, too afraid to swat at her, but she was a big, blurry blob in my vision. My eye fluttered as tears ran down my cheek.

"That's one of his names." She said it loudly like it was for the others and not me. "Greyvenhorn…" She let go and whipped back from me. "Kingsgard."

The voices erupted in hurried frenzy.

"It can't be." A blue light whined above me.

Beside me, an orange light said, "It could only be."

And then in unison I heard. "The Soulstone."

The violet fairy leaned against the tower. "We know why

you're here."

"Can you tell me?"

"Better. We can show you." She swung around one of the iron rods and opened a slot on the contraption. The light reflected through the device and projected an image on the wall.

"Fascinating!" I ran over to study the image but had to stand off to the side to stay out of the light.

The blurry image barely let me see anything more than a dragon and rider. I returned and studied the device. The fairy had opened the back. Inside gears, disks, and lenses filled the contraption. The teeth looked rough, unlike the perfect craftsmanship of the parts I was used to but the purpose was clear. Mother used a similar projector to tutor me.

"I think this is how it works." I fiddled with the contraption and closed the panel.

The fuzzy image on the wall disappeared and the fairies protested.

A small wheel on the side rotated the device to align the lenses. The image returned in crystal clarity and all the fairies cooed. Everything was displayed in silhouettes. Subtle changes in the disks animated the figures.

"That's better." I returned to the wall. The image of a rider stood beside a dragon. Dragon runes wound around the outside, I wasn't certain what they said but it was beautiful.

The clicking of gears hummed softly in the air and the image rotated to a castle half buried in the ground and hidden by trees. The fairies' wings fluttered and each began to glow with light. They whispered to each other and whipped up into the air creating a frenzy of fairies.

The violet fairy landed on the contraption. "It's never done this before."

I shrugged. "Is that the Arthurian academy?"

"Before all the stones fell down."

"Astounding."

"You humans need to become better builders – mountains rarely fall down."

The image rotated again and all the fairies zipped down to their mushroom chairs. A low "Ooooooo" echoed throughout the room. A king sat on a throne surrounded by dragons and knights with long lances. All the fairies shouted at once. "The Good King!"

"Is that the king who started the academy?" I asked.

"No. He's always shown with a sword in a stone. That's the last king. He was a good man. He liked fairies and always protected our home."

"What happened to him?"

She didn't answer, she couldn't take her eyes off the wall as light and shadows rotated and morphed into a different image. Londaria. Clouds spewed out from the bottom of the aircity leaving humans and dragons collapsed on the ground.

In their silence I clenched my fist. "Nothing I'd been told was real. The Cloud King–" The fairies hissed when I said his name.

"I was told he was a hero."

The violet fairy shook her head. "He killed his brother and kidnapped dragons to do bad things to them."

"He what?" I hadn't heard any of that. But I had seen the evidence. I pointed to the device. "What is this?"

"The last rider made it."

"Who?"

"Queen Boudicca hid here for a few years but sealed the doors and left."

"The lady from the statue."

The fairy nodded.

"Then what is this sphere of light?"

"A soulstone. The Queen's dragon was killed by the Cloud King. If you bury it in a mountain at the full moon you'll have a celestial dragon."

"Then why didn't she bury it?"

"The Peacecrafter needs it."

The who? Her words tumbled around in my head. Queen Boudicca wanted people to know the truth about the air-cities. But I already knew. I'd seen their experiments on dragons. How they steal their energy to power the city. It must have been her husband who was killed by the Cloud King.

I froze. These silhouettes told the story of my family.

# Steamtree

# Chapter 21

A voice cried out from behind me. "Is it time for the gift?"

All the voices started speaking at once. "The gift!" Around me the fairies repeated, "Gift, gift, give him the gift!"

A red light zipped around me. "The gift is *for* the Peace-crafter."

"What if he's not the Peacecrafter?" said a blue light on a mushroom.

"He doesn't look like a Peacecrafter."

"I think he's dreamy."

"He's too tall."

"He walks with spirits and dragons."

In unison they cried out, "Ask the spirits."

The wind whipped through the room, and I had to shield my eyes from the dust and debris. The fairies cooed and I saw movement through my fingers. Wings fluttered, buzzing all around me, until lights lifted off and swirled in circles. Tiny hands pushed against my back. As I looked up, some-one walked through the doorway and disappeared. I went to investigate and thought I saw the outline of a figure turn a corner.

The fairies pulled at my coat and pushed against my back. Dots of light darted forward sprinkling glittery dust behind them. I'm not sure if I had a choice to follow the tiny creatures, but whatever lay at the end of this hall pulled me by an invisible rope.

No ghost. I was disappointed, but my racing heart couldn't take much more. At the end of a hall covered in thick vines with tree roots growing down from above, a half-shattered statue held a folded cloth in marble hands. Half shattered, I could see the statue was of a man with a cape kneeling but nothing above the elbows survived.

The worn blue velvet cloth trimmed with gold, had a depression in the center. Fairies swirled around me and the statue. Buzzing high-pitched voices, I couldn't understand shut out the rest of the world. Out of a chaotic frenzy of zipping lights, three balls of light, one red, one violet, and one blue brought the soulstone and set it on the cloth.

With only my courage, I reached out and wrapped my fingers around the orb. Sparkling clouds of light swirled within the translucent sphere. The soulstone was warm, not hot, but pulsing with energy as if filled with magic. I picked it up and the orb pulsed scattering the fairies. I jumped, and bobbled the sphere in my hands, but pulled it against my chest so I wouldn't drop it. The chamber plunged into shadow.

"I can't just take this. That wouldn't be right."

A single violet light zipped into the chamber and landed on the shattered statue. "It's a gift for you, that's what she said."

"Who said?"

"The queen." She put her hands on her hips. "She sealed

this place. Set the contraption, and said this was a gift for the one who unsealed the academy."

"How do you know all of this?"

"I was there when she handed the dragon academy over to the fairies. Are you going to kick us out now?"

"What?"

"We just assumed you would reopen the academy and rip out all our hard work."

"Hard work?"

She pointed to the vines and the roots streaming down from above. "Looks way better doesn't it."

"It is lovely." I leaned down. "I'm not here to reopen anything I'm hiding from archangels and airships."

"But you brought a dragon."

"Actually, he brought me?"

"Oh." Her eyes lit up and she glowed brightly without even flapping her wings. "We get to stay! We really like it here." She flew up in front of my face.

"A soulstone."

"A gift for you, to place in the mountain."

"Thank you." I didn't understand any of this, but the orb was fascinating, and my mother had taught me to thank people for their gifts."

She swished back and forth. "You're welcome, but really it is from the queen so I guess on her behalf, you're welcome."

I smiled and the little fairy sped off.

The violet glow faded. I took a deep breath. Putting the soulstone in my bag and ran off to find IronCloud before I saw any other impossible things.

# Chapter 22

I skipped down the stairs so fast I thought my feet would fall out from under me. "IronCloud you have to see what I found."

The dragon lay where I'd left him in the center of the stables by the stairs. He slowly lifted his head, the corners of his mouth curling up in a smile. "What adventure have you been on?"

"I saw the queen, well a statue of the queen and then there was this contraption that told a story of the last king of the academy and there were fairies. They came to watch." I couldn't slow down my words. "They asked a bunch of questions and even considered making me go mad, but then the spirits gave me a gift," I held out my hands. "A soulstone."

IronCloud pulled back at first, but then leaned his head over me. He studied the orb with one of his large eyes. "It is." Excitement filled his voice. "Soulstones are powerful. The concentrated mana of a dragon."

"I know," I looked up at him, "But what does it mean?"

The dragon shook his head. "Destiny is a heavy burden."

I turned the sphere in my hands. "Actually, it's kind of light."

IronCloud chuckled. "We'll see." His head lowered until

he was just above mine. "There's something you have to do. To protect your father, your mother, and your friends."

"I'll do it." My heart beat faster, all I wanted was to help my parents, and the dragons.

"You need a new name." His head hopped to my other side. "One you can be known by among dragonriders."

"Your friends will call you Anderax but the world needs a name to call you."

I thought for a long time, running over everything from something strange like WrenchSword, or dragon sounding like IronFang. Perhaps I needed something simple like Mike or legendary like Arthur.

One name flashed through my mind, and only a few people in the world would know what it meant. "I know my name."

"That was fast, who are you?"

"Call me Steamtree!"

# Chapter 23

IronCloud didn't speak for several moments and then blurted out, "I like it!"

I sighed. "Good, because I had no idea how to choose another."

"It's a good name. A mix of the air and ground."

I hadn't thought of that, but he was right. Steam was water turned into air and trees grew up from the ground. "Can I ask you a question?"

"Always."

"Why did you bring me here? I don't think I'm worthy of all this. I'm just a kid from the aircities."

"You don't see what I see."

"Your eyes are ten times bigger than mine."

IronCloud's head threw back and laughed. His whole body shook. He lifted his paw and pinched the length of his nose. He slowed his laughter and leaned down next to me. "Did you not sneak out to follow the Nightraven?"

I popped up. "How do you know that?"

"I don't think she would have taken you along on a mission."

I shifted. "Yeah that's true."

"You also jumped off an aircity."

"Well, the archangel didn't give us much of a choice."

"You didn't freak out when you saw a dragon."

I nodded. 'You're astounding."

"You also helped out those two cadets on the outpost. They may not have made it off without you."

"That was you in the cloud." My mouth dropped open.

"Yes. You and others only see a boy. I see courage, wonder, and heart… I see a young dragonrider."

My breathing shallowed, and my heart pounded inside me. No one had ever said anything so nice. Everyone always tried to protect me, but this dragon saw what I could be, what I will be. I wiped a tear from my cheek, but I wasn't crying. *Something above me must be dripping.*

"There are truths about your life that you are not yet aware of. But more importantly you brought us word of the dragon's plight. I know that dragon."

I stepped back. "You do?"

"He is an old friend."

"Aren't you angry?"

"Of course." IronCloud settled back down "My rage is deafening. but foolish action would only get us all killed. Dragons do not live for a thousand years by being impulsive."

"Wow, that's a long time."

"It doesn't feel that way."

"I guess you get to see a lot of history."

"I do."

"Why don't you have a rider now?"

He lifted his head and looked around at the stables. "He was taken by an archangel."

I froze and my heart fell through my chest to the pit of my stomach. "I'm so sorry. I've seen them and wouldn't wish it on anyone."

"Worse, he saved me. The archangel tried to kill me. He was ripping my soul when my rider climbed out of his saddle." He paused and took a deep breath. "His last words – I was more important. I had to find and protect the Peacecrafter."

Sounds echoed through the stables. They came from outside in the forest. Then I heard the unmistakable roar of a dragon. IronCloud perked up and I ran toward the huge dragon door.

Three dragons landed in the clearing. Odin, Duncain, and Lady Z dismounted. They looked around and turned to each other, pointing toward the door.

I jumped. Odin and the others were okay. I ran into the clearing, into the sunlight. "You're alive! I didn't know if I'd see you again."

The dragonriders spun on their heels. "There you are." Odin pulled me close. Here I'm expecting to find a boy huddled and frightened in the forest but I find the extraordinary."

"I feared some of you might get hurt helping me."

Odin dropped to one knee. "We're fine, lad. How are you?"

Duncain kept one hand on the hilt of his sword and his eyes on the trees. "We've been worried what happened to you."

"IronCloud brought me here. I'm fine, better than fine. I got to climb a tree."

"Really?" Odin ruffled my hair, and looked over at Iron-

Cloud. "I'll have to talk to him about that."

"Sir." Lady Z pointed to the open door. "The academy's been opened."

Duncain shook his head. "That's impossible."

I pointed toward the tree. "I climbed up and unsealed the door."

"You opened the academy?" Lady Z's piercing green eyes stared at me through the slits of her visor.

Odin tugged on his beard. "By the spirits. It would make sense if it is Anderax, but it means he's imprinted with Iron-Cloud."

"But IronCloud hasn't imprinted with anyone since—" Duncain paused. "He can't think this kid is the Peacecrafter?"

Odin nodded. "He must. And he might be right."

I didn't understand what the fuss was all about. Anyone could have climbed up and used the key to open the academy door. *Couldn't they?*

We walked inside and were greeted by IronCloud's mischievous grin.

Odin stopped and put his hands on his hips. "We were all supposed to rendezvous in the forest and fly to the Highland Academy."

IronCloud shook his head. "My rider had another destiny."

"That was not your decision and what happened to talking about this before you imprinted?"

"You'll have to talk to the archangels about the timing."

Odin hit his palm with his fist. "That's why you should have gone to the Highland Academy. We were worried sick."

"My rider needed to be here."

"He's a boy. He's not a rider yet."

"Time is irrelevant. In the future he will be a better rider, but he is a rider now."

I smiled. "Thanks. That means a lot."

"He has already chosen a name, Steamtree."

Odin glanced at me and the back at IronCloud. "Oh, did he."

IronCloud bowed his head. "His path was set the moment he jumped off the aircity."

The headmaster pointed his finger. "But we agreed."

"I cannot lie to my rider, and it is better to test him now before he learns the myths."

"No one asked you to lie. We just weren't going to tell him yet."

That didn't sound right. "Tell me what? That Kingsgard once ran this academy. My mother's name was Kingsgard. I learned that upstairs."

Odin shook his head. "Oh, your mum is gonna kill me."

Duncain stepped up. "I should check the rest of the academy."

I put up my hand. "This isn't ours anymore. It's the fairies."

All the adults turned and looked at me. IronCloud chuckled.

Duncain started up the steps. "Well I'm just making sure there are no archangels." Two steps more and he ran into an energy barrier made of vibrant light. He jumped back and pressed his hand against the shimmering barrier.

"That wasn't there before." I said.

Odin ran his fingers through his beard. "I don't think they're going to let you up there."

"Who? The fairies?" Duncain let his hand fall.

"Exactly," I said.

Odin stepped out to the clearing. "We should get going anyway. All the riders are gathering."

I turned back to the stares and remembered the Soulstone. The fairies wanted me to plant it in a mountain, but never gave it to me. Looking at the stairs, sadness drained me. I feared I'd messed up. Maybe the fairies changed their mind.

I didn't want to leave. I'd never stepped in a more fascinating place. Every smell, every stone, and overgrown vine. This place gave me the same feeling as seeing the fort in my steamtree on the Caledonia. I guess home is the places where we belong. Plus, they had trees here.

# Chapter 24

I climbed onto IronCloud, and we flew in formation for most of the afternoon. I'd rather fly around and check-out the clouds, but I don't think dragonriders get to have fun.

Iron Cloud's wings stretched out and buffeted with the currents of air. We sat second in a wedge formation. My heart jumped every time we drifted closer to Odin's dragon. But IronCloud never wavered too far and held his place perfectly. Made for the sky, dragons didn't need us to fly, only to keep them in formation.

We emerged from the fog, into a hidden valley with a huge stone castle perched on the shore of a lake. The dark water of the loch looked still as glass, and tall grassy hills surrounded the entire area. A compound of buildings surrounded the castle. The dragons landed on a stone platform jutting out of one side of castle.

The second we landed, Odin hoped off his silver dragon, and yelled, "I want all these dragons prepped to fly! Riders, I want you all in the War Room in an hour." He pointed at me. "Steamtree I want you safe in a room." He grabbed Duncain's shoulder as he passed. "Escort him to the cadets. Hopefully they'll keep him out of trouble. Then have the watch doubled."

Duncain nodded.

Odin rushed off. Captain Duncain pulled off his gauntlets, and walked over to me.

"A dragon academy with real dragons." My eyes grew as I stared at the castle. My jaw dropped, until I noticed all the dragons watching us. I snapped my mouth closed. I wouldn't want them to get any wrong ideas.

Staring at these dragons, though, melted all those thoughts away. I was on the ground. I was standing in front of dragons. Sure, they looked like they wanted to eat me, but they were real. Not statues or decorations on a door. I'd even climbed a tree. Life was perfect.

The ground. I looked down at the stone. Which oddly didn't move, I'd never felt anything so solid. Everything in the air shifted, even the aircities adjusted to winds and turbulence.

Lady Z pulled off her helmet, revealing short dark hair. She pointed toward the dragons. "We only fly Great Dragons here at the Highland Academy."

"They are great, but I think they want to eat me."

Duncain leaned closer. "She's referring to their species. The type of dragon they are."

Olgarth nudged me in back and I stumbled forward. "Don't worry, you're scrawny, and wouldn't be much of a meal."

"Oh." I hoped that wasn't true, but I wasn't about to ask questions when I could feel the hot breath of Olgarth's dragon.

"Come on, I will introduce you to the cadets." Duncain

said and pointed toward the castle.

I followed him away from the dragon landing and climbed a long set of stone steps. Bits of grass poked through between the stones. I'd never seen anything like it. The aircities had perfect vegetation. Every blade of grass was cut to the same length. Every flower sat in an individual pot, and every bush or shrub had been shaped to perfection. Here nature was wild and unpredictable. The grass shot up in different directions, the stones were worn, and the flowers covered the land in large patches. I'd just come from a fairy tale, and hadn't left.

We crossed through a large stone gate. Dark mosses filled the cracks as vines wove their way along the castle walls towering on each side of us. Deep ruts in the ground followed the passage around to a courtyard with a large keep, or central tower, rising up and disappearing into the fog that began to envelope the valley. On one side of the courtyard a small house with four large doors sat nestled within the walls.

I asked, "What is this place?"

Duncain said. "The castle was built centuries ago. Dragons took it over after the destruction, and began training riders."

"Will my mother be able to find us?"

"Of course. She lived her when she was your age," Duncain pushed open a thick wooden door with iron hinges. "You're among friends, Anderax."

I didn't know too much about my mother's childhood, but I'd never heard she'd lived on the ground. "What about my father?"

"She went back for him, and soon we'll be going after the

dragons."

"Because of the dragons they have chained up."

He nodded. "That's right," but his expression faded. "And to bring the war to the aircities.

We entered a room at the end of a short hall where a small group of people about my age sat on couches around the fireplace. They fell silent. One boy jumped up and saluted Captain Duncain by placing his fist over his heart. My eyes grew, I stared at the boy from Skye Outpost. This kid's head cocked to the side, and I realized he was having the same thought I did.

"You." He said, pointing at me.

"The riders from Skye Outpost." I looked around and found the girl with long red locks holding another boy in a head lock. Her face flashed a stunned reaction, but she quickly replaced it with a raised eyebrow. She released the tall lanky boy who stretched out his neck and half-waved at Duncain.

"Oh good, you all know each other. That will make this easy." Duncain pointed at the boy. "Grif, this is our guest, and you cadets are going to hang out with him and make sure nothing happens to him. He has archangels after him, so cut him some slack." As Duncain walked to the door he paused. "I want all of you to stay alert. Orders will come tomorrow after we've figured out what the archangels are doing."

"I'm Grif." He pointed to a dark-skinned kid with curly hair. "That's Caster. "The guy with the goggles is Lockhart, and you met Serafina."

The tall guy extended his hand, "Name's Parsons."

"Are you okay?" I asked as we shook hands.

"Oh yeah," He nudged Serafina in the arm and said, "We were just… disagreeing."

She shoved him away, and pushed her hair back behind her ear. "Please, my dragon is so faster than yers."

"No way." Parsons raised his fists.

Serafina planted her feet and I thought they were about to fight, but a large boy, with a chest twice the size of mine rushed down the circular staircase in the corner.

He ran between Serafina and Parsons to seize Grif by his jacket. "Guys you won't believe this! I just talked to my dad. They got an air-dweller agent or something. How cool is that." He spun around and pointed at me. "Who's this?" He eyed me menacingly.

Grif brushed the boys hand away and said, "Captain Duncain said, the headmaster wants us to treat our guest nicely."

The large boy turned to Grif and hid his mouth with his hand. In the loudest whisper I'd ever heard, he said, "Who is he?"

Everyone's eyes turned to me. They all wanted to know the same thing, but my legs wanted to run. I wanted to make friends. I took a deep breath and said, "I jumped off the aircity with the Nightraven."

"Whoa! That's crazy!" Several of them said in unison. "That was you."

Grif slapped the large boy's back. "This is Olgarthson! He's the legacy, his dad's a rider."

"I met him. Kind of." I extended my hand and said, "I'm Anderax—"

"Stop!" They all blurted out. Grif smiled. "We don't use

our real last names at the academy. That way our families are protected."

"Call me Steamtree."

"Good to meet yah." Olgarthson held out a huge hand twice the size of mine. Was he ten or twenty? I couldn't tell. "You a cadet?" he asked, gripping my hand until I thought it would crumple like a piece of paper.

"No. Before today, I had no idea you all existed. I've only lived in aircities."

"Aircities!" Olgarthson smacked my shoulders as he gripped me and pulled me close. "You've lived on an air-city?"

"Mostly on my airship." My feet dragged across the floor, and Olgarthson must have realized he'd snatched me up because he dropped me. I almost fell, but pulled my legs beneath me.

Parsons mouth dropped. "You have an airship?"

"Yeah. The Caledonia. She's a dirigible."

Olgarthson nodded. "Oh, those are good ones."

"Thanks. I like the crew a lot too."

Parsons asked, "Did you see any battles?"

"Right before we landed in Londaria I saw dragons attacking a castle on top of a cliff."

"The abbey." Grif leaned forward.

Olgarthson smiled, tossed a walnut in the air, and caught it in his mouth. "My dad was there. He and WingBurn tore those airships to pieces."

The cadets surrounded me, each asking questions, one right after another. I spun around, right into Serafina. Curly red locks fell about her face and green eyes blazed behind them. "Have you ever seen an archangel?" She asked.

The image of those mechanical wings sent a shudder through me and I nodded. "Been chased by them." My throat closed up, making it hard to breathe and trapping my words deep within.

Olgarthson swiped his fist through the air. "Yeah right, he's pulling our legs."

"I am not."

Parsons' shook his head. "Next he'll say he's seen a mech-winger ripping souls."

"I have."

Everyone froze. Slowly, they leaned closer. I found it harder to breathe as if they used up all the air. I pushed my way past them and bolted toward the base of the stairs.

"Ease off him." Grif said as he pushed Olgarthson away. "You okay?"

"Yeah just needed better air." Thick and sticky like soup, each breath came with a drink of water. "How… do you people breathe this stuff?"

"What?"

Caster, the kid with the curly hair, nodded. "He's used to thinner air. He's a cloud dweller. Think about how the air changes as we climb." He pointed to Olgarthson. "Your dad complains about how hard it can be to breathe above the clouds. It makes sense he would have trouble down here where the air is thicker."

I nodded and tried to take a deep breath.

They might only be cadets, future dragonriders, The Scourges of the Sky but according to the nobles I should be trembling in terror from these dirters. However, the nobles had been wrong about everything else, maybe they were wrong about dragons and their riders.

"Enough questions." Grif declared. "We should take him around the academy. Where should we start?"

Serafina put her hands on her hips. "The rookery."

Caster said, "That's a great idea. The hatchings have been running around all week."

I was hoping they were talking about dragons the whole way down the stairs. When we reached the bottom Serafina pulled open a huge wooden door with iron hinges. I expected a dark dungeon, a place of slithering monsters, but I walked into a lavishly decorated chamber.

The rookery walls held nooks and niches chiseled with a craftsman's perfection. Some held clutches of leathery eggs. Others hosted dragons curled up on plush pillows. A few were large enough that only a head stuck out with the body within the wall behind it. The large chamber lit by several fire pits, was so warm sweat rolled off my brow. Dragons, none more than three feet long, ran around, flew back and forth, and clung to every surface. They looked like petite versions of the great dragons I'd seen earlier, four legs and two wings with long thin necks and tails.

Several attendants aided the young dragons, filling food bowls, changing water dishes, and I had to imagine there was a pile of dragon poop somewhere nearby.

Two little red dragons landed on my head. Their sharp claws pricked my scalp, but it didn't really hurt. A green and a blue dragon perched on my arms as I held them out to steady myself. It startled me, but I didn't flinch. What if they got spooked and shredded my face?

Grif pointed. "Looks like we have a dragonrider."

"Really?" I said.

Serafina had a dragon curled around her arm and scritched under its chin. "Dragons are very particular about who they associate with. You must have a true soul for them even to approach."

"Fascinating." No sooner had I spoken, when something slithered along my foot. I glanced down as a long snake-like dragon with no legs but two feather wings curled around my feet.

Grif picked up a red dragon about the size of a dog and set it on his shoulder. "Look at that even the plumed dragon likes him. What makes you so special?"

"I don't know."

"Grif don't be rude." Serafina reached down and ran her fingers along the ridges of the plumed dragon's head. "Don't listen to him. It's a rare breed from South America. He was saved from an air noble's kitchen. He's just trying to get warm."

"He can stay, I don't mind, I just can't walk."

Eventually they pulled the dragons off me, but more took the chance to land. Then the largest of the young great dragons walked over and leaned against my leg. I had to widen my stance or I'd fall over.

Olgarthson leaned around me. "He's a natural. They're clinging to him like he's made of meat."

That didn't sound good. If they tried to eat me, I don't think I could defend myself. "So how do you become a dragonrider?" They all shot each other glances and I wondered what was wrong. Had I asked something taboo?

Serafina handed off her dragon to an attendant and then helped free me. "You have to be chosen by a dragon. They choose their riders."

"What about these guys? They seem to like me?" A dragon climbed up over my back, used me as its launch pad and soar over to a nook in the wall.

Caster shook his head. "A dragon must be at least a century old before it takes a rider."

"So, all of you have dragons?"

Serafina nodded and so did the others.

# Chapter 25

We left the rookery, which was hard, and walked up the chipped, worn stones of the grand staircase. The stairs retained their grandeur, but the palaces in Londaria and Paris d'laire showed no age or wear, and were covered in plush carpets. I'd ridden the mechanical steps in LuftBerlin which climbed twenty-five stories from the courtyard to the airdocks. I didn't know which I liked better.

We wandered through the main tower to the stone balcony. The whole valley lay shrouded by a thin fog. "Why doesn't the headmaster live in the castle?"

"He isn't a king." Serafina lit up. "We rule ourselves, unlike the air-nobles and their queen."

We walked down a long hallway on the far side of the castle, and the air thickened with the strongest aroma. Caster held his nose, "We're above the dragon stables."

Grif pinched his nose. "I thought it was Olgarthson."

They all laughed but I didn't get the joke. I found the strange smell kind of sweet. "I want to see the dragon stables."

Grif pointed. "Yeah, there's a stairwell at the end of this hall."

I leapt down the stairs two at a time and froze as I reached the bottom. A cavern opened up in front of me, but instead of rough cave walls, polished stone and huge pillars held designs of colored bricks. Three large arches led to the landing platform I arrived at earlier.

Each dragon had a large square stall, the central section remained open for the dragons to gather. Streams meandered through the stables bringing water to every dragon. Several moved about while others curled up with their tails wrapped around them.

"Don't you feel the dragonfear?" Serafina asked. She didn't flinch, but Caster's leg wouldn't stop twitching and Parsons trembled as his eyes darted back and forth. "We're all learning to overcome their powerful presence."

"Really, I'm just excited." I rushed into the center of the stables up to a dragon with a broken horn. I raised my hand and said, "Wow, you're amazing."

The dragon eyed me and several others began to circle. The younger dragons came in a so many vibrant colors, but these dragons had darkened with age, and retained only traces of color along the edges of their scales.

I didn't feel any fear. In fact, I'd never felt better. I wasn't nervous, or scared. Confidence flooded every vain, and all doubt melted away. I reached out and touched the dragon's shoulder. The warm scales vibrated with energy and thumped with each beat of its heart.

I heard gasps behind me.

Caster said, "They're taking to him, same as in the rookery."

A dragon bumped me in the back, and I stumbled forward. His nostrils flared as he inhaled, and my shirt lifted off my back.  Another craned her neck over the others, coming within inches of my head.

I reached up and rubbed under her chin. I'm not certain why I thought it was a lady dragon, but she was slimmer than the others and, I don't know, she appeared to be a girl.

Leaving these dragons, I followed the cadets toward the back where their dragons lay. Caster and a three-horned green dragon dropped next to Grif and his red dragon. Caster had a bag of sugared walnuts. He ate one and popped a couple in his dragon's mouth. Parsons leaned into the stall and cupped his hands together. Caster tossed him a couple candy-coated nuts which he shared with his green dragon. The dragons perked up at the sugary smell and Caster passed around the bag.

"Tell us about the archangels." Serafina hopped up onto the half-wall between the stables as a sleek blue dragon lifted her neck to join us.

"Okay." I grabbed a sweet walnut treat and passed the bag to Serafina. "Archangels look peaceful but are really scary and intense." Everyone nodded, even the dragons.

"Have you seen them fly?" Lockhart asked as he leaned back against his dragon with scales as black as night.

"Oh yeah. They soar above the cities looking for trouble. Then they swoop out of the sky and snatch bad guys up. I watched an archangel lift a man, thirty feet in the air. He took his hand like this," I splayed out my fingers making a claw. "The weird white globe on his chest swirled with light which made the tips of his fingers glow, and he," I shoved my fingers against my chest. "Wrenched the soul from his body." My fist clenched tightly and I pulled away, lifting my shirt. If only they could see my memories. My story lacked the fear of that moment.

Grif gripped his chest. "Freakiest thing I ever heard."

"Those stories are real." Serafina shuddered. "Creepy."

Caster turned to his dragon. "I bet the globe is a Chi-amplifier." He turned to me "They were discovered in China centuries ago. They're called dragon pearls, because they were found with the wingless dragons of the East."

"Really, I didn't know that." The thought that archangels might be using dragon tech ignited a fire of anger within me. It wasn't right to use dragons for their life-force.

"Have you ever seen the Cardinal?" Olgarthson asked.

Parsons shook his head. "He doesn't know *everyone*."

I nodded. "I had dinner with him."

Olgarthson sat up. Grif choked on a walnut, and Parsons fell off the bench. Serafina cocked her head to the side and said, "Really?"

"Yeah. We were in Londaria, staying with the Duke, and the Cardinal came to dinner one night. He is a scary looking guy. His eyes don't show a good man but something darker."

The cadets looked at each other. Serafina's smile faded. "The Cardinal, the Lord High Chancellor, and the Queen form the unholy alliance that keeps the Wing Wars going."

I hadn't thought about that dinner, but to everyone around me, I'd dined with the enemy. The eyes of the cadets and their dragons, stared back at me. Was I an enemy or a friend?

"Until the Peacecrafter returns." Caster said, raising his finger.

Olgarthson chuckled and tossed another candy walnut in

his mouth. "Please, not the Peacecrafters again."

I leaned in, "Who"

Caster sat up, "The most powerful dragonriders were known as Peacecrafters. They'd become such great warriors they didn't need to fight to win battles."

Grif added, "But they haven't existed in a hundred years, and it's just a legend."

"Astounding." I took a risk and asked a question. "Can I ask about your dragons?"

Grif stood up. "How rude of us, sorry. Allow me to introduce InfernoWing." The red dragon bowed his head revealing rows of horns.

Serafina motioned to her blue dragon. "This is Sapphire-Sky, and she's the fastest dragon here." Her dragon nodded and lifted her forehead up to connect with Serafina's outstretched fist.

Olgarthson pointed to his big red dragon. The dragon lifted his head from the next stall and in a deep throaty voice said, "I'm MountainBlaze."

My eyes grew. I wasn't expecting the dragons to answer me.

A gravelly voice came from behind me. "They call me RidgeHorn, and sometimes I let Parsons' here hold on."

"Hey." Parsons laughed. "He couldn't land without me."

The dragon nudged him and knocked him off the bench. Grif tossed RidgeHorn a walnut which he gobbled down.

Caster leaned in. "This is EverGreen. He's super smart, but don't test us, we're kind of shy."

I nodded. "I think that's great. Being really smart."

Caster smiled and so did EverGreen.

If I didn't know better, I'd almost say they kind of looked alike. "Why are they different colors?"

Caster sat back against EverGreen. "Dragons originally came from different regions. The colors evolved to match the habitat. So, they can more easily evade predators."

"I never would have guessed that."

"Profound." Parsons laughed and turned to RidgeHorn. "All he needs to know is that dragons are dangerous, making them infinitely better than anything else."

We all laughed including some of the dragons.

I stopped. The image of the dragon chained up in Londaria flashed through my mind.

"I have to tell you guys something."

Serafina went silent and her eyes narrowed. "What troubles you? I can see it in your eyes."

The laughter trailed off. Grif, InfernoWing, and the others leaned closer as if they sensed my fear.

I looked at all of them, but the words were trapped in my throat. Maybe I shouldn't tell them. It wasn't for me to say, but I really liked the dragons and it was wrong what the aircities were doing. Plus, these cadets had befriended me, trusted me so quickly, maybe I owed them the truth. "Londaria is sucking the lifeforce out of a dragon to stay in the sky."

# Chapter 26

Silence. No one spoke a word, I barely heard any breathing. Even from the dragons whose eyes kept getting bigger until I could see the fire beginning to burn within. I shouldn't have said anything. I knew I shouldn't, but I just couldn't stop myself. A growl so low I barely heard it rumble the stall. All the dragons growled, as their rage built so did the sound.

Grif stood up and confronted me. "Do you know what you're saying?"

The cadets looked at each other, but Serafina jumped down from her half-wall perch. "Wait, does the headmaster know this?"

"Odin? Yeah, my mother told him."

She smiled. "Then we don't need to worry. The dragonriders are already on this. You know they won't sit back and let it happen."

Grif crossed his arms. "That's probably why everyone is in the War Room."

Olgarthson eyed me. "So where have you been? The headmaster had to fly off to find you."

"IronCloud took me from where I jumped, and we ended up at the old Arthurian academy instead of here."

Grif stopped. "Wait, IronCloud let you ride him?"

"Yep." I smiled. "He said I was a good rider too."

"He what!" They all said in unison.

"But that means…" Serafina covered her mouth.

Grif asked, "So what exactly happened at the Arthurian Academy?"

"I opened the dragon door and went inside."

All the cadets stared with open mouths, same as the headmaster, Duncain, and Lady Z had earlier today. Did they all know the legend?

Parsons' hit Caster in the shoulder. "Does that mean he's the…"

Olgarthson grabbed Parsons. "His dragon is IronCloud and he opened the Arthurian Academy. What else do you need."

"I don't know who I am, but the fairies said I was the Peacecrafter."

They all, "Ooooohhh," in unison.

Grif grabbed my shoulder and pulled me close. "Come one let's get up to our room, and you can tell us all about it."

I didn't want to talk about the academy yet. I didn't even know how to feel or what it meant. I stared out a window at the night's sky. Light danced as the clouds rolled in overhead. In the distance lights twinkled as if the stars had gathered in a single spot.

"Londaria." Staring up at the moon, I had the same ache in my heart as when I looked down at the trees from the Caledonia. The aircity was so far away. They'd been my world and now were nothing more than a twinkling light in the sky.

My muscles twitched as I thought about my parents, both

up on Londaria. I sighed. I had to find them. I was finally on the ground and all I wanted to do was go into the sky. *Life's weird.*

# Chapter 27

Serafina sat next to me by the window, and joined me in looking up at the large moon poking through the clouds. "Is everything all right?"

I pointed to Londaria blinking in sky above, "My parents are there."

"You're worried about them?" She shifted back and forth.

"I can't stop thinking about them."

She didn't say anything for a long moment. Maybe she didn't know what to say. I didn't. Finally, she said, "The dragonriders are looking for them."

"Except, everyone is here right now." I turned to her. "From the way Odin's talking, I fear they're going to attack Londaria."

"They have to respond to the dragon-knapping."

"I know, but it means a lot of people are going to get hurt. Maybe even my parents." A tear ran down my cheek, but I wiped it away before she could see.

"Nightraven might've rescued your father."

I sat up. "Maybe. But I have to do something."

"Wait, what?" She turned toward me.

"I have a dragon; I can get back to Londaria."

She shook her head. "What about the archangels?"

"If you come up from underneath, the wind is too strong for the archangels, but I bet a dragon could survive."

"You know a lot about aircities."

"I've been to most of them in the European skies. My dad's an airdrainium inspector. I'd always thought his job was boring. But he did teach me a lot about aircities." I jumped up. "I have to talk to IronCloud."

Serafina twisted on the branch and leaned over. "Wait, we have orders."

"I'll be back."

I found him curled up by a tree beyond the edge of the academy. From behind a thick tree trunk, I watched to make certain no riders were caring for their dragons. No one came. I was alone. As I tiptoed closer, IronCloud asked, "What are you doing here?" He didn't even open his eyes.

"How did you know it was me? Do we have a bond or something?"

"I smelled you. You're covered in dirt."

"Oh."

He opened his eyes and his whole body shook as he chuckled. "You haven't answered my question."

I whispered, "I want to find my mom and dad."

IronCloud's head pulled back. "Anderax, that would be dangerous."

"I know, but if we come up from underneath there won't be any archangels. I'm certain you can survive the winds, and then I can climb onto the city and do a quick search. If I run into any trouble I'll just do what the Nightraven did."

His head turned to the side. "Jump off and hope I catch you."

"Exactly."

"That was not part of her plan."

IronCloud leaned in staring at me with one eye. Then he flipped his head and stared at me with the other eye. "You're going to get me in bunch of trouble."

I pulled back and he got even closer.

He smiled. "I like trouble."

I sighed and smiled.

"Grab my saddle." He pointed to a rack by the other dragons. "Not knowing where the Nightraven is bothers me too."

# Chapter 28

I pulled the straps with all my might and buckled the saddle onto the dragon. I'd never put a saddle on before, IronCloud walked me through it. "How does that feel?"

IronCloud stretched and twisted. "Feels pretty good to me."

"Let's go." Stepping on his leg, I hooked my foot in the stirrup, swung my leg over and grabbed the reins. "How do we take off without being spotted?"

"Like this." IronCloud tucked his wings back and sprinted across the tor, or hill. Then he leapt into the air and soared out over the loch. The wind whipped against my face. I reached into my bag and pulled out my goggles. Once on, my eyes no longer stung, and the vast star-filled sky looked close enough to touch.

The academy faded into the distance, but I was in the sky again. I'd climbed a tree. I should be sitting on the clouds, but with my parents in danger it was hard to have fun. I stared at Londaira off in the distance.

"Where to?" The dragon asked in a deep grumbling voice.

I pulled the reins and directed him toward the aircity. He smiled and with two beats of his wings we sped faster through the clouds. I held on and tucked down like I'd seen the riders do.

IronCloud beat his wings a few more times and said, "Storms under Londaria, we'll have plenty of cover."

I nodded but realized he couldn't see me and I said, "I don't mind getting wet."

His belly rumbled against my thigh as he chuckled. My smile couldn't fade. With a dragon at my side I didn't fear the future. My parents lay ahead of me.

*     *     *

My back started to ache and I straightened up. The wind pushed me back, but I pulled on the pommel to keep me from bending backward. As I twisted the kinks out of my back, a blinking light beneath the clouds caught my eye.

Leaning closer to IronCloud I pointed. "What is that?"

"Looks like an airship, but we are far from the shipping lanes."

"It could be a spy keeping an eye out for dragons."

IronCloud growled. "We'll dip into the clouds just to be safe."

"Good idea."

We dropped into the puffy white clouds as we approached the dirigible. The airship even had exterior steam pipes. Same as the—my heart beat faster and I leaned over so far, I almost fell off the saddle. "The Caledonia!" I pulled on the reins. "Hurry and descend. That's my ship."

"Okay, but let's be smart about this. We'll pass by to make sure it's safe."

"They're probably looking for me."

We flew past the stern and I saw the familiar green painted letters that spelled out Caledonia. My steamtree fort lay nestled in the pipes, and the large circular window that sat in the living room. I didn't see the crew on the catwalks, but at this time of night they'd be in the galley singing and playing cards. I wanted to jump off, but IronCloud insisted on buzzing the bridge.

We flew alongside the bridge windows and I craned my neck to see inside. My mother stood next to Captain Campbell at the map table, and Brisco held the wheel.

I waived.

Brisco stumbled backward as his mouth fell open. The wheel spun and the ship began to twist in the wind. IronCloud spread his wings, and we lifted into the air. The ship quickly returned to normal, but my mother and several of the crew ran out onto the catwalks.

I shouted to IronCloud. "We need to get closer."

"You got it." He dropped and tucked in his wing a bit but the wind kept pushing us away.

"Close enough." The top of the Caledonia didn't look that far. It was made of a thick canvas and would cushion my fall. Below that lay the helium tanks, giant rubbery bags filled with gas.

Slipping my feet from the stirrups I took one last deep breath and pushed off. I heard a half roar from IronCloud, and distant screams from below. The rushing wind silenced everything. It pressed against me and whipped my coat about. My feet hit the top of the Caledonia, and I bounced off the taut fabric.

I rolled over my shoulders before spinning around and

sliding down the side. Each support beam just beneath the canvas skin bumped me further away from the airship. I flailed my arms trying to control myself. Ahead lay the catwalk. My feet hit the metal grating with a clatter, but momentum pushed me to the railing. Rohl grabbed the back of my jacket and I stopped.

"Thanks," I said as he let go. "Permission to come aboard."

Rohl exhaled with a sigh and ran his finger through his greasy hair. "Granted."

My mother pushed through the crew and snatched my shoulders. She pulled me close and clutched me so tight it was heard to breathe. "What were you thinking?"

"We saw you, and I had to come over."

"Who brought you here?"

"IronCloud." I said proudly. "He says one day I'll be a rider."

Her eyes grew. "IronCloud said this about you?"

I nodded.

She took several hard breaths. "We're going to have to talk about this, but for now let's get you inside."

# Chapter 29

We stepped inside, and the instant they closed the hatch, the wind disappeared. My clothes and hair stopped constantly moving. Pulling my goggles down around my neck I unbuttoned my jacket.

My mother took me down onto the bridge, "Captain."

He snapped to attention. "Yes ma'am."

"Carry on the previous course."

"Yes ma'am."

"Young man, follow me." She motioned with her hand.

I quickened my step so I was right behind her. Rohl waved and I did too, but I made certain it was behind my mother's back.

The heels of her boots clattered on the metal grating and with each step I started to think I was about to get grounded. All the bad things I'd been doing, sneaking off, getting chased by archangels, spying, becoming a dragon rider, flooded back into my mind—and then there were all the things she didn't know about, like the fairies or the soulstone. Maybe I should have stayed at the Highland Academy, because I was pretty certain I wouldn't be leaving my room for the next few years.

She entered the living room and spun around. I stumbled on the rug, and stopped. She wasn't looking at me. Her eyes darted along the ceiling above me. I'd never seen her act like this before. *How much trouble was I in?* I'd know from how many of my names she used.

"Anderax." She knelt down and rubbed my shoulders.

*Only one.* I didn't know if that was a good thing, or signaled this would be really bad. *Here it comes. Stand strong.* Hopefully IronCloud was close enough to lend me his strength.

"I'm sorry I had to leave the academy without you, but I had to learn what happened to your father."

"The headmaster explained that."

She nodded and took a deep breath. "There's something I should have told you before now…" She swayed back and forth looking at me. I didn't know why, but she hadn't started punishing me yet.  "Our family. Oh how do I say this?"

"I know."

"What? Who told you?"

"The fairies."

"Who?"

"They live in the Arthurian Academy and told me that the Kingsgard once ran the academy. Then I remembered you're a Kingsgard. You told me once when we spoke about formal names."

"Oh wow, you even sound like a dragonrider." She pulled me tight.

"I do?" My head dropped. "Don't be mad. IronCloud is the most astounding dragon/person I've ever met. He's so wise and makes all my fears disappear. But…" I paused. I didn't know how to tell her the rest.

"Everyone's calling you the Peacecrafter aren't they?"

I nodded and wondered how she knew so much. I didn't

even have to tell her anything. She just knew. Maybe mothers really did have special powers like reading minds and eyes in the back of their heads.

"Oh wow, this just got a lot more complicated." She smiled, and I freaked out a bit. "I should have told you years ago, but I wanted to spare you my troubles."

"I can handle it." My shoulders slumped. "Why are you the Nightraven, and why do you look like the Princess!"

My mother had lied, beat a guy up, and jumped off an aircity. I had so many questions they were just popping out. She didn't say anything, only stared off into the night. The moment turned into minutes, which stretched to awhile. Maybe I shouldn't have asked. Mothers and silence never mixed well.

"You saw the Princess?" She finally asked.

"She looks like you, but with blonde hair."

My mother wiped a tear from her eye, and nodded. "Before I married your father, my name was Beatrix Kingsgard, but I changed it to Aja Grayvenhorn. I'm afraid there's more to this than old names." She took several hard breaths. "It began long ago. After the great king's death, our family was given the academy to protect. We Kingsgard ran the academy for years, until we were betrayed."

"By the Cloud King. I watched a story about it."

She blinked and pulled back. "That's right, and then the academy was sealed."

"I opened it and saw Queen Boudicca, she reminded me of you."

Tears streamed down her face. I must be in a mountain of trouble, but instead, she whispered, "Oh my, could you really be?" I wasn't certain if that was a question aimed at me, but the she locked eyes with me and asked, "Who took you to the Arthurian Academy?"

"IronCloud."

"Sneaky dragon." She released a heavy sigh, and fixed the collar of my jacket. "You have royal blood. That's why dragons give you strength instead of fear. You see, the Queen of Londaria is my aunt."

"What?"

"My parents, your grandparents were the king and queen of Londaria."

I froze. A hundred questions poured into my mind. Maybe more.

"Fifteen years ago, my father's sister, your aunt, seized the throne."

"The Queen?"

"Yes." A harsh tone entered her voice. "She schemed with the Lord High Chancellor and Cardinal because my father wouldn't go along with abusing dragons. I was rescued and slipped out of the city. The headmaster took me in at the Highland Academy but I didn't do well in the structured world of the dragonriders. I snuck off at night to learn why the Queen had betrayed our family, and created the Nightraven to hide my identity."

Thinking of her at the academy almost made me chuckle. "That's why you didn't want to meet the Princess."

My mother nodded. "There is one more thing, about the Princess."

"Who is she? The Queen never had a king?"

"My twin sister."

# Chapter 30

I said, "You're a princess!"

My mother shook her head. "No, to the aircities, I died with my parents."

"But you are."

"True, but the lavish life was never something I craved. You've seen her. The Princess is a prisoner in a golden cage."

"But you could be the ruler of the aircities."

She pulled me close and hugged me tight. "I'm only concerned with finding your father."

"Me too." I laid my head on her shoulder, but snapped up. "And we have to free the dragon."

"We'll see what we can do."

I nodded and my mouth stretched open in a yawn.

She bopped my nose with her finger. "It is late. Way past your bedtime."

"I don't need a bedtime."

"Even dragons have bedtimes. Now wash up, brush your teeth and your ears. Then I'll tell you a story about the Nightraven."

I bolted off to get ready.

*     *     *

The next morning, my mother came in to wake me, but I sat at the window. "What do you see?" She asked.

"The trees."

"Did you finally get to see one up close?"

"I climbed one to get into the academy."

Her smile grew. "I'm so glad."

"Can I go to my steamtree fort before breakfast?"

A dark shadow rolled over the Caledonia. The dark shape was so big that it darkened the surrounding clouds too. My mother and I looked up and saw a huge airship with cannons sticking out every few feet.

"A dreadnaught." My mother gasped. "The most dangerous ship in the air armada."

I couldn't take my eyes off the ironclad airship.

"They're above us. They're going to attack." She bit her lip as she thought.

Two puffs of smoke popped out of the dreadnaught, as twin grappling hooks connected to steel cables arced down and latched on to the Caledonia.

"Stay here, and hide." My mother ran out of my room.

If I was going to hide, it wasn't going to be here. I ran for my fort. The crew ran around as I found the hidden entrance to my steamtree under the pipes.

"What would IronCloud do?" I asked myself.

He'd prepare to be boarded. He'd defend his friends. I was going to be a dragonrider someday, I might as well start today. I might not be able to fight the soldiers. They were bigger, and had guns, but I could make it difficult to take control of the Caledonia.

# Steamtree

I darted through the pipes and climbed up into my stream-tree.

# Chapter 31

I went to a porthole and peered outside, but stayed close to the edge so no one could see me. Six men slid down each zipline and landed on the catwalks. Several crewmen ran out to greet the soldiers, including Dogger, who slammed his giant wrench into a soldier's helmet.

Rohl stepped out below me. He had a heavy chain twirling like a propeller. A soldier snuck up from the stern of the ship, behind Rohl. There must be another zipline at the back of the Caledonia. Rohl didn't notice the man, his eyes never left the fight at the bow. The soldier raised a club. A section of thick pipe lay beside me on the floor of my steamtree. I was going to use it as a base for a telescope, but this was more important. Opening the porthole, I picked up the heavy pipe and hung out the window. Wedging my feet against the wooden boards, I took aim. Letting the broken pipe go. It slammed onto the soldier's helmet, and he collapsed like a sandbag.

Rohl spun around and grabbed his chest. He looked up, and I waved.

I wiggled back inside the porthole. Soldiers might be on the port side too. I darted to the other window where I spied another soldier walking along the catwalk.

He stopped in front of the steam overflow vent to check his gun. If I could get to the lever, I could blast him right off the Caledonia. I grabbed the door handle in the floor and slowly raised the hatch. I peered through to make sure he hadn't moved. Climbing down the ladder, I reached for the lever on the edge of the platform. In the whipping wind he'd never be able to hear me, but if he turned, he'd definitely see me.

The soldier struggled with the bolt of his gun.

My heart pounded, but my fear faded. Could IronCloud be nearby?

The soldier closed the bolt and raised his rifle. Out of the corner of his eye he saw me, and I yanked the lever. Hot steam blasted a cloud which surrounded us. I saw his arms flail and heard a fading cry. The winds whipped the steam cloud away and the catwalk was empty.

The crew fought them on both ends of the Caledonia. I looked up and saw the Cardinal in red battle armor and flowing crimson robes, sliding down the zipline. I had to tell someone. I popped open the nearest hatch, jumped through, and started to run down the corridor. I stopped, rushed back to the hatch, and locked it behind me.

My feet pressed hard into the metal grating as I ran through the airship. I swung around pipes to turn corners, and ducked under a couple of pipes to slip down to the next level. I checked my mother's workroom and bedroom. Nothing. As I rushed out onto one of the catwalks, I found her fighting a soldier. A skilled warrior, she didn't need any help.

A cackle pierced the noisy wind behind me. I spun around

and the Cardinal gleamed in his red battle armor. He pointed at me. "With the brat, she will do as I command."

The hatch lay too far away. I wouldn't have time to get inside and lock it. A small ladder ran up the side of the airship. Dogger and some of the other mechanics used it to access the top decks. The ladder was no wider than my foot, but I scampered up. I glanced over my shoulder and saw the Cardinal climbing behind me.

The wind on top of the Caledonia was stronger than anywhere else. My legs buckled in the intense breeze, but I ran along the spine of the Caledonia. My steamtree lay in front of me, but it was far away and behind hot steam pipes.

Laughter echoed behind me. "You have nowhere to go, son."

"I will not be taken without a fight." I reached into my bag and patted the soulstone.

"Get over here boy, or I will rip your soul from you."

"I'm not afraid of you." I held firm and said, "We can find another way, a peaceful way."

The Cardinal cackled. "Foolish lad, peace will come when the last dragon is chained in an airdrainium chamber."

"Peace will never come if you give pain to dragons!"

# Steamtree

# Chapter 32

The Cardinal charged across the taught canvas roof of the airship. Steel-tip claws on the ends of his armored hands swiped at me, but I ducked. My heel caught one of the airship's ribs and I fell backward against the hull.

I scrambled backward on my butt trying to get away from the armored Cardinal. He snatched my foot and I kicked his hand. He twisted me over and lifted me into the air. I was upside down, but that didn't bother me. He might have my leg, but the rest of me was free. I reached into my bag and pulled out the soulstone. A bright white light flared. The Cardinal shielded his eyes and screamed in pain. The Cardinal let go and I fell to the canvas.

Rage exploded from the Cardinal's eyes as he back-handed me, and I soared off the Caledonia. As I flew backward, I saw my mother scream and reach out. She climbed on top of the airship. I couldn't hear her, but watched as she ran to the edge. She dove off the edge, and I reached out for her, but an archangel soared up behind her. The mechanical-winged figure snatched her right out of the air, and threw her back up on the Caledonia.

I fell too far to see any more. The Caledonia faded into

the distance. Normally this would be the part where a person would panic. A normal reaction to falling, knowing a big splat came  at the end. I didn't have that. Without the noise of the engines and fighting, I was left with the peaceful wind, like flying on a dragon.

I plunged through a layer of clouds, and as I popped out the other side I realized why. IronCloud. I flipped over as the dark shape burst through. His wings folded back, he dove for me. I flattened out, and grabbed hold of the saddle. Straining my muscles, I pulled myself over and wedged my feet in the stirrups. IronCloud spread his wings and we soared back into the clouds.

My cheeks inflated as I forced the heavy sigh out of my chest.

IronCloud glanced back. "You okay?"

"Yeah, I'm fine, but we have to get back. My mom is in a fight with the Cardinal."

IronCloud roared. "I have something I'd like to say to the Cardinal."

We burst through the clouds and found the two airships still locked together. "There they are." My mother fought with the Cardinal. Keeping his claws at bay with her sword. Her face lit up as we locked eyes, but the Cardinal used her distraction to pick her up and toss her off the airship.

I screamed.

The Cardinal pointed to the archangel, and he flew off after my mother.

Panic ripped through me like a wildfire. What if he was going to rip her soul? I couldn't let that happen. I pulled the reins and we darted over the ship after my mother.

IronCloud growled. "Ready yourself. When we get closer to the archangel he'll flare his wings and attack."

My chest tightened. How would I fight off an archangel?

My mother flailed her arms a couple of hundred feet away. The closer we got to the archangel, the more he glanced over his shoulder. Then he flared his wings.

This was it. The archangel's wings billowed, and he spun toward us. I leaned back against the saddle. The archangel's wings loomed above me. I thrust the soulstone into the air and a pulse of light knocked the archangel away. The gears and struts on the archangel's right wing twisted and bent, sending him spiraling away.

IronCloud focused on my mother. I tucked the soulstone back into my bag and tucked up against the saddle to maximize our speed.

We swooped down, and IronCloud snatched her in his claws.

I thrust my hand in the air. "We did it!"

The dragon roared. I pulled on the reins and we soared back up toward the Caledonia.

My mother climbed up IronCloud's leg. She pulled herself onto the back of the saddle and secured herself with a strap.

I twisted to see her. "Are you okay?"

She nodded.

Relief washed over me, and I returned to the reins. Now we needed to help the Caledonia.

My mother leaned closer. "Where are we headed?"

"Back to the Caledonia."

"We need to get away."

"But we have to help the Caledonia."

She looked down at me. "All right, but we need to lead the dreadnaught away before it destroys the Caledonia." As we flew up the side she pointed. "You and IronCloud cut the grapplers. I'll deal with the Cardinal."

I shook my head. "We have it covered."

"What?"

I didn't answer. We crested over the top of the airship. The Cardinal pointed at my dragon and yelled for his soldiers.

IronCloud snorted. "I can't use my fire. I'll hit the Caledonia."

"Smack him." With the reins tight in my hands, I pointed and yelled, "Pass on the right, and tail whip him."

IronCloud roared. We rushed forward, banking toward the airship. Instead of plowing right through the Cardinal, we passed him. The Cardinal was set for direct attack, and looked confused as we passed. IronCloud whipped his tail, slamming into the Cardinal's chest as a loud crack echoed across the sky. The armor indented, and the Cardinal soared off into the empty sky.

I had no time to celebrate. We banked left, and Iron Cloud tucked one of his wings back to avoid crashing into the Caledonia.

I hoped the Cardinal would fall to the ground, and go splat, but a pair of mechanical wings popped out from under his armor, and he soared up to the dreadnaught.

My mother placed her hand on my shoulder. "We need to cut the grappler lines and set the Caledonia free. More soldiers are about to zipline down."

IronCloud spread his wings, and we charged the cables. I turned in my saddle and asked, "What can cut a cable?"

"Try my sword. Get as close as you can to those cables."

IronCloud soared closer to the airships, the tip of his wing almost scraping the hull.

My mother's focus never left the thick rope, swaying in the wind. We twisted with the air currents and banked to dodge the Caledonia. The sword struck and a twang like a broken guitar spring rang through the air. We turned toward the next rope, and she swung her saber. The front of the Caledonia was free.

"Let's cut them all!" I said, pumping my fist in the air.

# Chapter 33

IronCloud roared. We flew in front of the Caledonia's bridge and saluted the captain. He nodded back, and we soared around the airship. My mother stood up and prepared to strike the ropes connected to the stern. A strong wind pushed us off our line. We were going to miss the rope, but IronCloud turned on his side and thrust his back up. My mother swung her sword and sliced the rope as we flew by.

The cannons on the dreadnaught opened fire. Cannonballs soared over our heads. IronCloud chuckled. "If we stay below the airship, it's hard for them to aim."

"One more cable to go," I said.

The Caledonia struggled to break free. The dreadnaught pulled up and the cable rose above us. What if the dreadnaught was turning to fire on the Caledonia? My mother unhooked herself and stood on the dragon's back. As we slipped under the cable, she hooked it with her sword and it snapped in two.

The Caledonia raced away, embracing its freedom. Without the weight of the Caledonia, the dreadnaught sprang higher into the sky. The same as when I'd tumbled backward playing tug-of-war with Rohl and he let go.

IronCloud dropped into the clouds, and we flew off. I

scanned the sky and saw an airship heading out toward the sea. I pointed. "There's the Caledonia."

My mother touched my shoulder. "We're not going back. The captain knows what to do."

I paused. I didn't know what to say. I wasn't ready to leave. Every time I got someplace I suddenly had to leave again. "I don't want to go."

"The Caledonia is too exposed. You don't want them getting hurt do you? We're going to let them hang over the ocean for a few days."

That made sense, and I really didn't want anyone else getting hurt because of me. I nodded.

"Remember, if you need somewhere to go, the Caledonia will be northeast of Londaria."

"I will."

She leaned toward the dragon's head. "IronCloud, find us a place to land. We'll need a cave."

He nodded, and we soared toward the ground where a lone grass covered hill stuck out of the plain. As we circled, I spotted a large cave at its base. IronCloud saw it too and we set down on the loose rock in front.

My mother slid off, and I dismounted. IronCloud sniffed the entrance of the cave then turned and said, "I don't smell anyone."

"Good." My mother nodded toward the cave. "Let's get inside before the dreadnaught flies over."

She stayed at the entrance and watched the sky. IronCloud filled the passage and I explored the back of the cave. I opened my bag and the swirling light of the soulstone poured out. I aimed my bag to illuminate the cave. Large boulders made up the walls and ceiling of this central passage.

I hadn't spent a lot of time on the ground, maybe nature was more complicated than my tutors taught. Outside stood a large hill covered in green grass with a single tree growing at the top, but inside, looked like people made this place.

I spun around to ask IronCloud, but he stared at my bag and my mother still stared at the sky. I walked deeper into the cave. The passage led to a small chamber that appeared to mark the center of the tomb. The room had eight walls, and was big, I couldn't touch both sides if I extended my hands. A stone sat in the center with a bowl carved on top.

*Weird.* The fairies told me to put the soulstone in the center of a mountain, and it would create a celestial dragon. Here was a passage tomb that looked like the perfect place. Could I put the soulstone in a man-made mountain? How would I know if this was the place? I kind of wanted to keep it. I had already been saved a couple of times by its power. Maybe it could help me win this battle. Or worse, what if I was captured, what horrors would use to corrupt the soulstone.

If this was the perfect place, maybe it was meant to be. A Peacecrafter should know, but I was filled with doubt. *Trust the fairies. Trust IronCloud's instincts, maybe he landed here for a reason. He is a tricky dragon.* I took the orb from my bag. The soulstone fit perfectly on top of the small pillar. I stepped back and paused. The globe of liquid light was beautiful. I wished I could keep it, but if what the fairies said was true then this was going to grow into a celestial dragon. I didn't know what that meant, but I hoped I'd be here to see it.

A cool breeze whipped past me. I heard water and turned to see a small opening half the size of a doorway. Crouching, I shuffled along as this passage lead to the other side. I walked out on the back of the grassy tor. Before me, a deep scar, or gorge, had cut into the ground. A stream flowed into one end, but didn't come out the other.

I walked over and peered over the edge. A waterfall crashed down and a stream cut through the bottom before disappearing into the rock. I kicked a couple of pebbles at my feet, and they bounced down the side before splashing into the stream.

The water fizzed and bubbled sending gusts of air shooting up around me. I reached down next to my foot and picked up one of the small silvery stones. My father had a similar pebble in his office, encased in glass it sat on the shelf behind his desk.

*Airdrainium.*

I'd found airdrainium.

I spun around wanting to share my discovery but I was alone. Then IronCloud walked around the mountain with my mother on his back. I raised my hand. "Look what I found."

They did not look amused.

# Chapter 34

My mother slid off the saddle and landed on the ground in front of me. "Anderax what have I told you about wandering off. If it weren't for Iron-Cloud's impressive sense of smell, we may not have found you."

I held out the stone. "I found airdrainium."

"I highly doubt it." She took the piece from my hand and studied it. She even sniffed it. From the way she stared at her palm, I knew I was right. "Where did you find this?"

"On the ground." I pointed to the pebbles along the rim. "They're all over the place."

She stepped to the edge of the gorge and picked up a few of the stones at the edge. "It's the old mine."

"What mine?"

IronCloud answered, "Two hundred years ago an English nobleman discovered airdrainium, and unlocked the secret of levitating technology. He mined all he could, from the only known source in the world."

My mother nodded, "He was going to sell it, but the Cloud King double crossed him, and seized all he had. The nobleman was arrested, but refused to give up the mine's location."

"So, the King Cloud never found this place."

"Many have tried," My mother said. "All the airdrainium that has ever been came from right here. That's why they're running out."

I looked down at the pebble in my hand. "If there is more airdrainium, the aircities wouldn't need to use dragons for energy."

IronCloud nodded.

My mother went silent.

IronCloud sniffed the air. He hopped higher on the mountain and stared off to the north.

I wondered what he sensed, but my mother asked first, "What do you see?"

"Dragons."

I ran up the grassy side of the hill. "Are they searching for us?" I looked off and saw dark dots on the horizon. A lot of dots, skimming the tree tops and rising and falling with the land.

"I don't think so. They aren't flying a search pattern." Iron-Cloud's voice deepened. "They're headed toward Londaria."

My mother joined us on the side of the hill. "Odin was never going to wait for me. He's going to attack Londaria."

IronCloud snorted. "I need vengeance just as the head-master, but this isn't the way. Many dragons and riders might die."

I didn't want anyone to get hurt now that we had a solution. With new airdrainium shipments, the aircities wouldn't need dragons. No one would have to fear the aircities. I ran back to the gorge.

I heard my mother call for me, but I didn't listen. I filled my bag with the pebbles, and any larger chunks I could find. Maybe I could be a Peacecrafter. I would charge right up to the Queen, my great aunt, and tell her to let the dragon go. I'd found another way. She'd have to listen to a long lost Kingsgard.

IronCloud's shadow swallowed me, and I realized where my confidence came from. "Good idea," he said.

"Thanks."

"Let's get going, Peacecrafter."

I spun around and nodded. "Can you read my mind?"

"With a smile that big, I don't need to read your mind to know what you are thinking."

"That's not a no," but he was right I couldn't stop smiling.

My mother sat on the saddle. "Come on, we should join the rest of the riders."

I stepped on IronCloud's thigh and jumped onto the saddle. With my feet secured in the stirrups I pulled on the reins and imagined the perfect takeoff, using the tor to get some height to our jump.

IronCloud stretched out his wings to get ready for flight. He burst forward, charged up the mountain and leapt off. We soared up to the clouds and burst into the moonlight.

I loved to fly. The way it shook my stomach up. How the wind pressed against me. The freedom to go wherever I wanted. I'd lived my life on airships. Every day spent among the clouds. Between dragons and airships there was no comparison. Dragons were my favorite. Airships rarely touched the ground. They bobbed along the winds like clouds you told where to go. Dragons bridged both the land and sky.

We dove through the clouds. I reached out to feel the silky

moisture on my fingertips. We dropped below the clouds and right into a flight of dragonriders. IronCloud plunged past them and then we soared back up between the drag-ons looking for the lead formation. We slipped up above the headmaster. Odin cupped his hand around his mouth. "By thunder, my heart can't take that."

My mother yelled back. "You were supposed to wait for me."

"I could only keep this many riders on the ground for so long." He shrugged.

I patted my bag, "There's nothing to worry about. I'm going to make peace."

From the look on Odin's face I don't think he believed me.

# Chapter 35

I turned to the formation on my right and the cadets. If the cadets were included, everyone was here.

Odin drifted closer. "Nightraven, stay with the cadets." He pointed to my friends. "They'll be dropping some surprises on the airdocks and Cathedral."

IronCloud whipped his head around. "What! You're putting me out of the action with the cadets."

Odin shook his head. "It's not like that, you're carrying passengers!"

"I have the Peacecrafter and Nightraven." He snorted. "We'll do as we want!"

"We have a plan," Odin pleaded. "While riders engage the archangels, the cadets will drop bombs on the military docks and Cathedral."

IronCloud growled. "Not my plan."

"I have to agree with my dragon. My plan is to find the Queen."

My mother grabbed my shoulder. "No, that is not the plan."

"Queen, dragon, Dad." I raised a finger for each point. "But I haven't worked out the order yet."

She shook her head. "No, I am going after your father.

You and IronCloud are going to pick us up."

"That's a good idea." I nodded. "You go after dad, and I'll free the dragon. Then we go talk to the Queen."

"No. She'll be guarded by too many soldiers, the Lord High Chancellor, plus the Cardinal and archangels. We aren't here to dig up old family history."

"It's the only way to peace."

She gestured to the headmaster, "Odin, can you talk some sense into him."

"Now you see my problem," Odin laughed. "It's too late to plan now." He pulled back. He and his dragon soared higher into the sky. "Begin the attack runs on Londaria."

The sound of dragon horn trumpets rang through the sky. Lady Z and Duncain pointed. I looked up and above Londaria, the Fleet hovered in a line. War Zeps, dreadnaughts, and airskiffs dotted the sky as archangels hovered between them. Duncain waved his hand and his formation soared off to engage the Fleet.

Odin motioned toward Londaria, "Get close to the buildings. It's the only way to avoid the cannons."

All the dragons rose high into the sky until, they crested at the top of their arcs and dove on Londaria. Bells rang throughout the city, alerting every one of our attack. The two sides smashed into each other in a ferocious battle. Archangels darted among the dragon formations, and the dragonriders stuck to no less than a three-on-one strategy. The airships' cannons belched smoke and fire, as chaos erupted in the sky.

We followed the cadets and soared toward Londaria.

Each of the cadet's dragon had a strange contraption on

the back of their saddles. A set of mechanical arms holding a teardrop shaped bundle of cloth on each side of the dragon. Grif led the charge and lined up on the air docks. Each cadet peeled off from the formation and banked toward the military airship docks. Diving to gain speed they pressed hard with their feet, triggering the mechanical arms which flung the bombs. The bundles exploded on impact sending fireballs into the sky.

My mother pointed toward the palace, "That's where we need to go."

I nodded, pulling the reins to the right, or starboard. We raced between the tall buildings, the tips of his wing almost clipping the buildings. The palace stood like a fortress on the riverbank. Spires rose into the night, their flags flapping in the whipping winds. Soldiers lined the battlements and an archangel hovered above.

I patted my dragon's neck. "We can make it, IronCloud."

"Yes, we can." IronCloud flapped his wings and we sped faster. His muscles twitched underneath me. Did instinct tell him to bank, but then why wasn't he? I was the rider, I was the one with the reins, and if I wanted to charge an archangel he would follow without question.

When his muscles twitched, I pulled the reins. We darted down a side street and swept around the archangel and soldiers. We didn't fly straight or level. We banked up and over the buildings. Turning quickly to charge the palace's battlements. The soldiers fled in terror.

IronCloud banked around one of the palace spires and dove for the main hall. "It's not over yet." We landed hard on the balcony. IronCloud's claws tore through the thin layer of stone and the metal underneath.

My mother slid off and spun around. "You both get out of here."

I reached out. "No, I'm coming with you."

"Anderax, I am your mother and I'm telling, it's too dangerous. Take IronCloud to the edge of the battle and wait for a signal that I have your father. Then come back for us."

"But that's not my plan.

"Anderax, I can't go after him if I'm worried about you." She touched my leg. "IronCloud get him out of here." He didn't answer, and she ran off toward the door.

I didn't like it one bit, but I couldn't just defy her.

IronCloud craned his neck around. "I don't listen to mothers. Only my rider."

I wanted to hug him. "Okay, but if we get grounded… you're doing the chores with me." I nodded toward the main hall. "Let's find the Queen."

Movement behind the stained-glass windows snatched my attention. Soldiers ran toward the door my mother had slipped through. They ran along a balcony and below on the main floor I saw the hi-nobles pressed up against the windows, and in the center stood the Queen.

I knew what I had to do. What the Peacecrafter needed to do.

I wanted to take IronCloud in with me, but he was too big. "Can you get me inside?"

"One door coming up." The dragon smashed his head through the glass, and tore the thin walls open with his horns. "Pardon us your Highness, but this young rider would like to speak with you."

The hi-nobles screeched. Rushing against the walls, they huddled in small groups. The Queen and her attendants pulled back in fear. I ran up IronCloud's neck and stopped atop his head. He lowered me down, and I jumped off, landing in the center of the hall. As I approached, the Queen regained her regal composure, fixed her crown, and sat on the throne.

"Thank you." I nodded to IronCloud. "He's my dragon. He's really nice. Pardon my entrance. I know this isn't proper."

The Queen trembled but firmly said, "No, it is not. I hope the dragonriders are not led by children."

I smiled. "No, I'm just a cadet."

IronCloud snarled. "He is hardly just a cadet."

I wiped my face and half-turned back, "Don't embarrass me in front of the Queen.

"I want to tell you who I am, but for now, just call me Steamtree."

As I looked over the hi-nobles, I saw Duke Skylark and the Duchess, who even wore one of my mother's dresses. Near them, the Princess stood behind a soldier.

"Steam-tree?" The Queen asked.

"That's me. You see, I'm from both worlds." I turned to address the hi-nobles, hoping to ease everyone's fears, and open their hearts. If I could change open one person's mind, it would be a start. "Did you all know, as I do, that the ground isn't infected with plague and that the aircities are in danger of falling as the airdrainium runs out." Whispers erupted in the crowd of nobles. "But I bring hope."

"Hope?" The Queen leaned forward.

"Yes," I saw the Princess step forward, and from the Duchess' shocked expression, I was pretty certain she remembered me. "I see a world where dirters and air-dwellers live in harmony."

Soldier rushed into the chamber as the Cardinal burst through the doors. His red armor underneath his crimson robes. "Do not listen to this boy!"

IronCloud roared, silencing the room and freezing the soldiers in place. "You will listen to the Peacecrafter."

# Chapter 36

The Cardinal's narrowing eyes, turned to the Queen. She was the one I needed to convince. I eased my expression and said, "I need you to listen, and not just because I have a dragon."

The Cardinal pointed at me with a steel-clawed gauntlet. "Your Highness, allow me to have this criminal taken away."

She shook her head. "He is only a child, Cardinal. Surely Londaria's threats do not come from someone so young."

"You do not know who he is your Highness. He is dangerous, and needs to be contained."

"I've lived in the aircities, and I've been to the ground. I even climbed a tree, a huge oak." I motioned to the hi-nobles behind me. "The people on the ground are good people, but they fear the aircities as much as nobles fear the plagues."

My mother burst in. "Anderax!" She kicked a soldier in the face and ran to my side. She grabbed my jacket and pulled me behind her.

The Queen's hand covered her mouth as her eyes grew. "Beatrix? It can't be, you're dead." Her eyes darted to the Cardinal and the Lord High Chancellor.

"You killed my mother and father, but your men missed me."

"My brother betrayed our way of life. He would have let Londaria fall!" She pointed to the giant diamond on her chest. "I saved this city."

I stepped out from behind my mother. "At the cost of a dragon's life. That isn't right."

The Cardinal whipped his robes out. "Those filthy beasts pushed us up here."

"No," I said. "The Cloud King's greed pushed them into the sky. He broke the peace."

The Cardinal's armored foot clattered against the marble floor. "Don't listen to these liars, your Highness."

"My son isn't lying. If you are looking for liars, start with your trusted advisors, my aunt. A Cardinal whose been trying to kill me for years, and a Lord High Chancellor so corrupt he is richer than the crown."

The Queen asked, "How could you know such things?"

"I am the Nightraven." She eyed the Cardinal. "The thorn in your side."

I smiled. The Cardinal spun around cursing under his breath. The Queen's eyes grew even bigger, but her shoulders slumped as her tough exterior shattered. The Lord High Chancellor's expression hardened. Everyone else in the room stood in stunned silence. In the back, I saw the Princess staring at my mother with tears trailing down her cheeks.

"Seize them." The Cardinal screamed.

The soldiers didn't move. They shifted toward the Queen, but her shocked expression didn't change. The Captain of the Guard turned to the Lord High Chancellor who pointed at my mother. Several soldiers stepped forward and lowered their spears.

"Stop!" The Princess ran forward pushing through the soldiers. "What is going on here?" She stared at my mother and spun around to confront the Queen. "I don't understand, you said my sister was dead."

The soldiers raised their weapons.

"Is that why you make me dye my hair? So, I don't look like her." The Princess walked up to my mother and me. "I thought… I dreamed you." She threw her arms around my mother, who hugged her back. Tears flowed down both their cheeks. "What have they done?"

My mother wiped her eyes. "They have my husband."

I added. "They're also using dragons instead of airdrainium. Which is really mean, and not smart."

One of the soldiers leaned over the Queen and asked, "What are your orders Highness?"

She hesitated but sat up straight and said, "Arrest them all."

The Princess whipped around on her heel and her dress swirled. "How can you arrest my sister?"

"You will pay for what you did to our father." My mother glared at the Queen with a look that usually came with the harshest scolding and weeks of not leaving my room. "I'm not here to ask twice. Where is my husband?"

The Cardinal snarled, "I should have killed you both when I had the chance."

The Queen shook her head. "Don't say that. It was a miracle that Beatrix survived."

"A miracle? It was Odin." The Lord High Chancellor shook his head.

The Cardinal pointed at him. "Hold your tongue Rycroft, or I'll send you into the afterlife."

"Oh please, you haven't been able to rip souls in years." Lord High Chancellor Rycroft turned to the Queen. "He fought Odin with the twins in his hands. The Cardinal dropped one to save his skin when it was certain the dragon-rider would defeat him."

"You dropped my sister!" The Princess cried.

"And they've been trying to kill me ever since."

"I would have succeeded if his greed hadn't stopped me." The Cardinal pointed his clawed gauntlet at the Lord High Chancellor. "The money your Highness provided to hunt the Nightraven, he adds to his personal accounts. He's been stealing money since the beginning."

The Queen's face twisted in horror. "Arrest them all!"

The Cardinal erupted. "I made you! It was my idea to get rid of your brother and seize the throne."

The Lord High Chancellor stepped forward. "Your Highness, arrest them and Londaria will be as it has been. We are your allies."

The Princess eyed the queen. "I see now why you've kept me caged. Revolving my friends every year so no one got close. Coloring my hair so no one would recognize my sister. Hiding her from me. Tell me who killed our parents, your brother, the true king of Londaria?"

The Cardinal's wicked smile grew. "It was her, only royalty can kill a king."

The Queen said nothing. Her gaze dropped into her lap.

The Princess dropped to her knees.

I raised my hand, "I have the answer."

"A child." The Cardinal pointed at me. "Impossible, another Nightraven lie."

My mother lifted her sword. "Stay away from my son."

"I'm here to end the wars. If Londaria had more airdrainium you wouldn't need dragon mana. My father is an aircity inspector. I know Londaria is already slipping. Skye Outpost, wasn't attacked by dragons. It fell into the sea because they ran out of airdrainium. Dragons are powerful, but their magic is not ours."

The Queen stared at me through narrow slits. I didn't like her expression. Normally, I'd start to doubt whether I was having an effect on these people, but with IronCloud looming above me I had no worries.

"Let the dragon go, and I will help Londaria."

"Londaria would crash by nightfall. That's what this is really about." The Lord High Chancellor pointed at my mother. "She said so herself. She was rescued by a dragon academy headmaster. They've waited twenty years for the perfect opportunity to strike. Now as we sit here listing to this child, they will send our beloved city crashing to the ground just like the outpost!"

I spun around. "The dragonriders didn't do that."

The Cardinal drew his sword. He rushed up to me and knocked my mother away. He pointed the sword at my chest. IronCloud tensed, and my mother reached out. The Cardinal screamed, "Dragons are the enemy!"

I held my stance, calling on all the courage IronCloud could give me, "No, dragons are wise. Humans broke the pact."

The Cardinal thrust his sword at my chest. Several nobles including the Duchess gasped. My mother cried out, and was grabbed by a soldier. She knocked him to the floor. IronCloud took in a deep breath. I raised my arms and fell backward.

Thunder rumbled across the sky, and rattled the windows, but no rain fell outside. In the distance, a beam of brilliant shimmering energy shot high into the sky. At the base of the pillar, light shone through the cracks in a lone tor. *It couldn't be the soulstone, could it?*

Everyone in the hall fell silent. We stared out the windows at the column of light in the sky. A translucent dragon, with a body of shimmering energy burst from the beam. Huge wings spread out, dripping particles from the wingtips and tail like embers in a fire. The Cardinal wobbled and turned, staring at the light. His sword missed its mark.

The energy dragon with a long comet-dust tail, soared toward the city. Every noble ducked and some screamed as it passed through the buildings. A blinding light filled the hall and particles of energy dissipated around us. Most people turned away with their eyes tightly shut, but I couldn't stop looking. I knew exactly what I was seeing – a celestial dragon.

The celestial dragon smacked the Cardinal, the Lord High Chancellor, and the soldiers knocking them all to the ground. After passing through this chamber, and the city, the energy being shot off into the night sky, becoming one with the stars.

By far the biggest dragon I'd ever seen.

"The amount of mana is astounding." The Cardinal sprang from the ground and spread his double mechanical wings. "Seize them!"

IronCloud snapped his jaws and bit off one of the Cardinal's four wings. "Leave flying to the dragons."

The Cardinal tumbled to the floor. He pulled himself up and threw back his robes. "I will kill that dragon. I will kill all dragons!" Smashing through the soldiers, he ran out the hall.

"He'll kill us all." The Lord High Chancellor gathered up his long black robes. "I must get my gold off this city."

Panic rippled through the room. As the Lord High Chancellor pushed people out of the way, the whispers grew even louder. My mother chased after the Cardinal.

"Everyone hold!" A voice cut through the room like a sword. All the hi-nobles stopped and looked at each other. We all glanced at the Queen, but she was silent. Her eyes trembling with terror.

"Take the chancellor into custody." The voice was strong, held no hesitation, but had a calm softness. The Princess stood and brushed off her dress. She wiped her eyes and walked up to the Queen who cowered against her throne. With the same confidence my mother showed holding her sword, the Princess grabbed the crown from the Queen's head. "You do not deserve the responsibility of running this great empire. You killed my father. I should do the same to you. I believe my sister came here to finish you, but I also remember a kind woman who took care of me. Which is the real you?"

The Queen's voice cracked. "I always cared for you like a—"

"Do not say that word! I know exactly who you are, for I too remember the woman who came to me that night. You lied. Committed a horrible crime, and used me to justify your reign."

"I am Queen of Londaria," she said cowering in her throne.

"No. You were regent, and used the Lord High Chancellor and Cardinal to change your title. I am the rightful heir of this throne." The soldiers snapped to attention. As the Lord High Chancellor pushed through the last of the nobles, the guards at the door crossed their spears and seized him. The Princess turned to me. "I know where they are holding your father. I will have him freed immediately."

"Thank you. But the Cardinal! He's going to kill the dragon." I ran up to the Princess. The royal guards shifted but didn't stop me. *Probably the giant dragon behind me.* I pulled a couple of stones from my bag and placed them in her hand. "Here. Have someone verify this is airdrainium. I know where more is, and I will gladly tell you if you'll end the Wing Wars. Specifically, the battle going on outside."

"I will."

"Good. I have to save the dragon. It's been really great meeting you." I climbed up a pillar to the balcony. IronCloud lowered his head and I jumped on. Running down his neck, I headed for the saddle. "Come on, I know a shortcut."

# Chapter 37

I leaned forward. "If we fly underneath, I can beat the Cardinal and my mother to the dragon."

IronCloud nodded. "It won't be easy, but we can do it."

"First we have to avoid all the archangels and soldiers."

"Leave that to me." IronCloud zipped through the city using the buildings as cover.

I pulled my goggles up over my eyes as we reached the edge and dove over the side. Thick clouds rushed out from exhaust vents on the bottom of Londaria, creating strong winds, and making the aircity appear to sit on a billowing maelstrom. We wove through the underside, banking steeply to avoid the downdrafts. We found pockets of stable air between the vents. I searched around the giant tanks and miles of connected pipes that created a web underneath the steel plates for the balconies my mother and I had jumped off.

The twisted railing of an inner balcony drew my eye, and I pulled the reins that direction. "There!"

IronCloud pumped his wings, and we soared up toward the balcony. He strained against the strong winds but couldn't get any closer. We were still too far for me to reach.

I had to save the chained dragon. "We can't be stopped

now."

IronCloud roared and banked away. He circled the edge of a vent using the wind currents to gain speed and slingshot up to the city. Instead of coming up from below he would come in from the side. "Get ready, you'll have to jump."

Pulling my feet from the stirrups, I knelt on the saddle, but held on to the reins. I kept my focus on the balcony. IronCloud snagged the crumpled railing and dug his claws in to the metal. I jumped and tumbled onto the balcony. Looking around I didn't see anyone, but the sound of soldiers running on the metal grating echoed nearby.

I turned back to IronCloud. "Stay safe, watch out for archangels."

"Me? I have it easy. You need to be careful. The Cardinal will be tricky."

I nodded and ran off.

The long hallways all looked the same, but seeing the numbers on the wall I remembered I needed D-3.

The thought of what the Cardinal might do pushed me harder. I ran faster, ignoring the aches building in my legs. Nothing bad was going to happen to that dragon. He had suffered enough.

Reaching the end of a hall, the painted letters across the top of the doorway told me I'd reached the right place — Airdrainium Reactor. A thick time lock had been placed over the door. A glass window on the lock showed the gears and spinning wheels inside. A set of numbers spun down with each tick and tock. Meaning it could only be opened at a certain time of day.

How was I going to get through? There was a keyhole.

The Cardinal probably had one, but if I waited for him, it would be too late. If IronCloud were here he'd burn right through, but I didn't have his strength. I was small and didn't have fire breath.

I looked around and saw the vent above.

*I am small. Perfect.*

Jumping as high as I could, my fingers gripped a group of pipes running on the wall. Reaching for the corner of the vent cover, I popped it off, and pulled myself inside.

The circular space was tight, but I had enough room to wiggle.

The walls were thicker than I thought, so I had to shimmy through a tricky tight turn. Light poured in leading the way to the next vent. I pushed off the cover which was only held on by thin metal tabs. The metal clattered as it hit the floor. I poked my head out to see if the guards had come, but all I saw was the dragon. I wiggled out and dropped down to the floor. Big gas lamps with huge reflector plates on the back circled the dragon, flooding it with light.

The dragon pulled against the chains, even in its weakened state. Longer and with bigger wings than IronCloud, I was like a tiny mouse standing beside him. However, like a mouse I moved without being noticed.

The light blinded me when I stood in front of the reflectors. I ran around the lamp and found that the reflector could swivel on the upright pole. I tried to push the large metal disks, but they seared my fingers and didn't budge. A large wrench and crowbar leaned up against one of the lights. I grabbed the wrench, and secured it to a large bolt on the back of the reflector pole. I pushed with all my might, the bolt turned, and the reflector plate moved.

As a shadow crossed the dragon's scales, its giant head slipped out of the light. The large eyes blinked, and as the last lamp was aimed away, a look of relief overtook the dragon.

I studied the chains. They were thick like the moorings lines on an airdock. I pulled on one. It was so heavy I only lifted a few inches before it slipped out of my fingers.

With soulful eyes, the dragon stared at me. Afraid it wouldn't like me, or trust me, I feared he'd lurch or attack. He remained calm and watched every step I took. The large eyes showed no excitement, as if this dragon knew I wouldn't be able to help. Several locks the size of trunks held the chains within huge rings bolted to the floor.

I didn't have much time. The Cardinal and my mother would be here at any moment. I didn't know what to do and I couldn't ask IronCloud, my mother, my father, or any crew member of the Caledonia. Just me and a dragon so thin I could count his ribs.

A lock needed a key and I didn't see any in this room. With my luck, the Cardinal had it, but this dragon needed me now. I picked up the crowbar and the dragon tensed.

I held up my hand. "No, no. I'm here to free you." I thrust the crowbar into one of the locks.

"Stop you fool!" I jumped as the Cardinal's voice echoed through the chamber.

# Chapter 38

I didn't turn around, or listen to the screaming Cardinal. I twisted the crowbar and heard a click. I pulled but couldn't move the thick metal lock.

Over my shoulder, I saw the Cardinal leap from the balcony, spread his three wings, and soar toward us. The Cardinal drew his sword. He aimed his blade at me, and swopped down. I dove to the side and tumbled along the ground.

My mother rushed in and grabbed the railing. "Leave my son alone!"

"Nightraven!" The Cardinal swopped back up toward the ceiling and pointed his sword at my mother. "This is all your fault, you evil wench."

She drew her sword. "I'm not the one with evil in his heart."

"I am a man of god you, you—"

"You hurt dragons." I pointed at the Cardinal. "They look fierce with sharp teeth and long horns, but they're smarter than us, and you're the one whose heart is black."

My mother smiled, but the Cardinal ignored me.

Normally that would upset me, but if he wasn't paying attention to me, I could continue freeing the dragon. I grabbed the crowbar and ran to the next lock. Metal clinking against metal drew me back to the balcony. The Cardinal's wings flapped as he slashed his sword. My mother stood on the railing blocking every strike.

I wanted to help, but I had to free the dragon, besides she didn't need me.

Jamming the crowbar into the lock, it caught on something inside, and I turned. The lock popped open. I tried to move the chain but couldn't. Would any of this even help?

The dragon turned his eye to the next lock. I nodded and rushed over, using the crowbar to unlocked it. Again, I couldn't lift the chain. I counted three more locks. The first two opened easily while my mother fought the Cardinal. They yelled at each other, but I couldn't hear them over the swords and machinery.

My mother flipped off the balcony and landed on the floor. Her shadow cast large on the wall by the turned gas lamps. The Cardinal dove after her. Hovering just above her, they locked swords.

The Cardinal pressed down on my mother's blade. "I'll finish what I started when you were a baby and the throne will be mine!"

Her knees held and she forced him back. "You could have killed my aunt at any time. You don't want to rule. You want power. Dragon power."

He roared, flapped his mechanical wings, and rushed her.

She twisted out of the way. "I bend with the wind…"

The Cardinal crashed into the floor and broke his wings. He leapt to his feet. My mother emerged from the shadows behind him and her shining sword poked through his shoulder.

She leaned closer. "And strike from shadows because **I am the Nightraven!**"

He shoved her back, and the sword tore out of his shoulder. He tossed a small bronze sphere at her. It popped open and four cables shot around her. She fell back bound by this device. He ran toward me as I plunged the crowbar into the last lock. The Cardinal snatched me up and shoved his hand against my chest. "Stay back or I rip his soul."

My mother struggled and used her sword to slice the cables. Her expression hardened. I'd only seen that look a few times. *He was in trouble. She'd be using all three of his names.*

She started walking toward us, and the Cardinal backed up toward the door.

The dragon pulled up his arms and the locks popped one after another. Chains whipped around the room and shattered the gas lamps. My mother dove under one chain, and I lost my crowbar as it fell from the lock and skittered across the floor. The Cardinal held me firm, and lifted me off the floor. The dragon stood up, and flung off the chains. His jaw opened and he bit down on the Cardinal. The armor and wings save the Cardinal's live, but one tooth punctured the orb on his chest and the shimmering gold liquid squirted out.

The Cardinal dropped me, and screamed. I ran toward my mother as the dragon whipped his head and threw the Cardinal through the wall. I ran to the hole and on the other side lay nothing but open air. I couldn't see the Cardinal in the night sky, but he didn't have a way to fly.

The dragon used its sharp claws to tear open the wall beside me. Its large head turned to me. Soft eyes closed, and his head bowed. I returned the gesture and saluted like a dragonrider.

The dragon pushed through the wall and soared off. Once free I heard every other dragon in the sky roar with delight. The sound was deafening and probably frightened all of Londaria, but a large smile crossed my face.

We'd saved the dragon.

# Chapter 39

My mother came up behind me and hugged me tight. "We're going to have to talk about what you're allowed to do until you're older." I squeezed her.

Before we could run out of here, soldiers filled the chamber. With the scowls on their faces and long poleaxes held at their sides, my heart quickened. My mother pushed me behind her and raised her sword.

A sweet smell filled the chamber, chasing away the stench left by the dragon. The Princess swept in flanked by guards, and the room brightened. I wondered if she'd been captured but she turned to one of the soldiers, and said, "Captain, you may depart and leave me with my sister."

"We shall remain outside, your highness." The soldier bowed. With a quick spin of his hand he ordered the others to leave.

The Princess walked over to us. "I have to confess I've never been down here before."

My mother lowered her sword.

I stuck my head out from behind her. "This was the airdrainium chamber, but they've been keeping a dragon locked in here for years."

"That's horrible." The Princess ran her hand over the

chains. "I stopped off on the way here." She motioned toward the door, and my father stepped through.

Even with a torn suit, he still walked with the proper stance of a nobleman. He lit up when he saw us. My mother and I rushed to his side. I wrapped my arms around his waist. She grabbed his neck, and they squished me between them.

The Princess' voice, choked by tears, said, "I've missed so much."

My mother walked over to the Princess and hugged her tight. "Thank you."

With a stunned expression, she wrapped her arms around her sister. "Of course."

The room lurched to one side, and the chains slid across the floor. We all remained upright, but had to take several steps to keep from stumbling. "What was that?" I asked.

My father's eyes grew. Without airdrainium, Londaria is going to fall, we have about…" He started using his fingers to calculate. "Three hours, your highness."

"We can't evacuate in so little time." She turned to me. "You said earlier that you could save my city."

I reached into my bag and pulled out several stones. "Airdrainium." I dropped them into my father's hand. "I even know where to find more."

"Unrefined airdrainium." My father leaned in. "With this in my hand we could power Londaria for weeks."

I smiled. "I'd be happy to show you where there's more."

My mother motioned to the chains. "The generators were removed to make room for the dragon."

My father perked up and raised his finger. "There are secondary chambers. Every aircity has three. A main and two backups. The Lord High Chancellor's been having me inspect them to avoid letting me see the main chamber."

The Princess asked, "Please, help me stop my city from falling any further."

"The chambers are to the north and south along the main axis. If the generators are filled with heavy water, then all you'll have to do is add the stones."

"We must go at once." The Princess touched his arm. "Please assist my city, Inspector. In truth, I'm not certain who I can trust at the moment."

"Of course." He took my mother's hand. "We'll be just a moment."

"Go. I have to contact the dragonriders and let them know what's happened."

The Princess spun around. "You're not leaving, are you? I was hoping we could talk. Half the throne is yours."

"No. I do not want to be a queen. I'm a dress maker."

A thump that shook the floor drew everyone's attention to the hole. IronCloud stuck his head through. "Did we win?"

"IronCloud!" I ran over and put my hand on his nose. "The Cardinal fell."

"And I missed it."

We laughed and turned back to my parents. My dad's eyes were the size of saucers. He pointed. My mother crossed over, and whispered in his ear. His eyes darted from me to her and back again.

I waved. "I'm a dragonrider!"

The Princess smiled. "He's the Peacecrafter."

# The End... of this adventure!

# Acknowledgements

First, I have to thank the Earth for growing trees. Plus, making them climbable and able to hold houses is such a great bonus. Much of my childhood was spent in the branches of the trees.

Thank you, to my wife, Amber. She's an amazing woman.

I must always thank my writing partners, and give them credit for the good words. They are all great authors and I highly recommend their books. Cole Gibsen is a young adult fantasy, T.W. Fendley is a young adult science fiction author, and Jennifer Lynn is a Celtic fiction author.

Did you see the amazing illustrations from Jennifer Stolzer, and that cover!!! She is a great artist, and I couldn't be happier with the work she produces! You need to go see more of her art at www.jenniferstolzer.com.

I also have to thank the literary groups I am a part of — St. Louis Writers Guild, the Society of Children's Book Writers and Illustrators (SCBWI), and The Write Pack, listen to me talk about writing every week on Write Pack Radio.

Many thanks to Emily Hall and the staff at Main Street Books.

I also, have to thank the one who thinks he's my muse, but he did spend most of this book in my lap… my cat.

Mostly though, thank you to all of you, the readers. I hope you enjoyed this adventure.

## About the Author

Brad R. Cook, is the author of *The Iron Chronicles* (treehouse publishing group) and *Steamtree: The Airdrainium Adventure* (Broadsword Books). A former co-publisher and acquisitions editor for Blank Slate Press, he is a member of SCBWI, and currently serves as Historian of St. Louis Writers Guild after three and half years as President. He learned to fence at thirteen, and never set down his sword, but prefers to curl up with his cat and a centuries' old classic.

Find more BradRCook.com

@bradrcook

# Read more from Brad R. Cook

The Iron Chronicles
Iron Horsemen
Iron Zulu
Iron Lotus

*High Adventure in the Age of Steam and Steel*

Plus check out these short stories
A Clockwork Heart
The Dragon Slayer
Doomed Flight of the Majestic

Find them online and at bradrcook.com


For discussion questions please visit the streamtree page at bradrcook.com